Match Wits with Super Sleuth Nancy Drew!

Collect the Original
Nancy Drew Mystery Stories®
by Carolyn Keene

Available in Hardcover!

Celebrate 60 Years with the World's Best Detective!

THE CLUE OF THE VELVET MASK

Carson Drew portends his teen-age detective daughter's future adventure when he says half-jokingly, "Nancy, don't let any of the party thieves ruin your evening."

The masquerade party at the Hendricks' mansion quickly turns into a mystery when Nancy and her favorite date, Ned Nickerson, spy a stranger about to climb the rose trellis to the second story. Who is this enigmatic man in the black cloak and the exotic woman in the Javanese costume? Are they members of the gang of wily thieves who sneak into parties given by wealthy people and steal jewels and art treasures? And why is the owner of the black velvet hooded mask that Ned finds in the Hendricks' garden so desperate to get it back?

To find the answers Nancy and her friend George Fayne devise a daring plan. The two girls switch identities! George soon discovers that while it is exciting to play amateur detective it can be dangerous to masquerade as Nancy Drew.

"Now let's see you tell the police what you know!"
the woman said

The Clue
of the
Velvet Mask

BY CAROLYN KEENE

GROSSET & DUNLAP
Publishers • New York
member of The Putnam & Grosset Group

Printed on Recycled Paper

Acknowledgement is made to Mildred Wirt Benson, who under the pen name
Carolyn Keene, wrote the original NANCY DREW books

Contents

CHAPTER I

Suspicious Masquerader

"You look lovely, Nancy, and very mysterious," said Hannah Gruen, housekeeper for the Drew family, as she smiled fondly at the slender, titian-haired girl.

Nancy had just finished dressing for a masquerade party. Costumed as a Spanish señorita, she wore a red gown with a long sweeping skirt and a black lace mantilla and carried a matching mask and fan.

She was glancing at herself in a mirror when her father, tall handsome Carson Drew, a criminal lawyer, walked into the living room.

"Bewitching!" he exclaimed. "And don't let any of the party thieves ruin your evening."

Nancy's blue eyes peered at him eagerly. "Dad, tell me what you mean."

"All right. The police are looking for a gang who rob homes while a party is going on. A masquerade would be an ideal place for them to carry out a theft."

"Oh!" exclaimed Mrs. Gruen. "It sounds dangerous."

"Now, Hannah, don't worry," Nancy said, giving the woman an affectionate hug.

Nancy's mother had died when she was a little girl and the housekeeper had lived with the Drews ever since. Both Hannah and Mr. Drew were very proud of the many baffling cases eighteen-year-old Nancy had solved.

"I hope the thieves show up tonight," Nancy said. Dropping the fan and mask into her father's hands, she put on gold hoop earrings.

"Ah! Now you're really a siren," Mr. Drew teased. "By the way, where is Ned? He'd better get here soon or you'll both be late."

Ned Nickerson, a college student who dated Nancy, was to take her to the party at the Hendrick estate in River Heights. Gloria Hendrick had been one of Nancy's school friends.

As Nancy glanced anxiously at the clock, the doorbell rang. "There he is now!" she exclaimed and ran to open the door. She greeted the attractive football player with a sweeping curtsy.

"Wow!" he exclaimed with a quick intake of breath. "You look terrific, Nancy! What a getup! I'm sorry I'm late. I had to drive Dad and Mother to the theater. Wish they could have seen you first."

"Never mind the compliments." Nancy laughed, pulling Ned into the living room. "I have a costume for you. Please change quickly."

"Not so fast! Do I have to go in fancy clothes?"

"Now, Ned, you promised. Besides, you'll like the outfit. Linda Seeley selected it personally."

"Who's Linda?" Ned demanded suspiciously.

"We used to go to school together. She now works at the Lightner Entertainment Company."

Nancy produced a large cardboard box, opened it, and removed an eighteenth-century Spanish grandee's costume.

"Isn't it marvelous, Ned? A plumed hat and high-heeled boots! A white neck ruff, too, and lace cuffs!"

Ned gave an indignant snort. "You expect me to wear that?"

"You'll make such a distinguished-looking escort," Nancy coaxed. "Please, Ned."

"Oh, all right," Ned acquiesced with a grin. He went to the upstairs guest room and ten minutes later appeared on the stairway landing. Assuming a theatrical pose, he asked, "How do I look?"

"Cool," Nancy replied.

Self-conscious, Ned came down the stairs to help Nancy with her cloak. Mr. Drew walked with them to the young man's car.

"If Nancy involves you in a mystery, Ned, be careful of those rented clothes," the lawyer said jokingly.

"Ned, Dad says we should keep our eyes open at the party."

"What's up?" Ned asked.

"If you've been reading the papers, you may know that thieves are suspected of sneaking into parties given by wealthy people living in the River Heights area. Thousands of dollars in gems and other valuables have been stolen."

"You think they may show up at Gloria's party?" Ned asked.

Mr. Drew shrugged. "I'm advising you and Nancy to be on the alert. The ringleader must be an unusually cunning crook," the lawyer went on. "He and his gang have been eluding the police for months."

Nancy and Ned assured him they would be on the lookout for any troublemakers. Then they drove directly to the Hendricks' home.

The gala affair was in full swing when they arrived. Dancers filled the ballroom which blazed with light from crystal chandeliers.

"I don't recognize anyone," Nancy declared as they watched the masqueraders.

A short-skirted ballerina and her escort in a minstrel suit danced nearby, doing the latest steps. Pierrot and Pierette sailed past, then a wooden soldier and china doll.

Presently Ned and Nancy were recognized by two of their closest friends. The two rushed over

Assuming a theatrical pose, Ned asked, "How do I look?"

to greet them. Bess Marvin, a slightly plump, blond girl, was dressed as a Southern belle. The other girl was Bess's cousin George Fayne. With her slim figure, George was convincingly disguised as a pageboy.

"Hi!" she exclaimed enthusiastically. "It's a wonderful party, but the dance floor is packed."

"Any villains here?" Nancy asked, and told her friends of her father's warning.

"Oh, how dreadful!" Bess exclaimed as her escort Dave Evans joined them.

"If there are any thieves here, they're masked," said George. "Just the right kind of party for a mystery, too."

"Oh, stop it," Bess begged, and offered to show Nancy and Ned where the checkrooms were.

She and George led the way upstairs, together with Dave and George's escort Burt Eddleton. After they had left their wraps, Nancy suggested pausing a moment in the second-floor library to look at the art treasures.

The room contained many valuable paintings, antique vases, and a priceless collection of miniatures in a glass case. Some were solid-silver figurines; others, portraits painted on porcelain. One of these, a likeness of Marie Antoinette, was especially attractive. Nancy noticed that the case was not locked.

"This is just making it easy for a thief," she remarked.

"Not so loud or you'll have a detective at our heels," Ned cautioned.

"I doubt that there's one in the place," George replied. "Gloria's parents never seem to worry about their valuables."

"Oh, let's forget robberies," Bess pleaded. "This is supposed to be a gay party."

"Right!" approved Ned, seizing Nancy's hand. "Let's dance!"

For the next half hour the young people had a wonderful time. The music was superb and Nancy forgot everything but dancing. Later as she paused, Nancy saw Linda Seeley standing near the refreshment table. The girl was not in costume, and obviously had attended the party as an employee of the Lightner Entertainment Company. Nancy took Ned over and both lifted their masks.

"Oh, hello, Nancy," Linda greeted her. "Did you approve of the costumes I sent out?"

"Perfect. The party's lovely, too." Nancy introduced Ned.

"I'm glad you're enjoying it, because I planned the party—or rather my company did. I wouldn't be here tonight except that my boss, Mr. Tombar, couldn't come at the last minute. I do hope everything goes all right."

"Of course it will."

"The truth is, we didn't expect so many people."

"Crashers?" Ned asked.

"I'm afraid so. We warned the family to be careful to admit only guests who could present invitations, but they didn't want anyone checked at the door."

As the June night wore on, the ballroom became very warm. Seeking the cool air outside, Nancy and Ned sat for a while on a garden bench. Then they decided to dance again. As they rose, Nancy searched in vain for her mask.

"I must have dropped it somewhere on the path," she declared.

Quickly they retraced their steps. The mask was nowhere in sight. As they searched for it near a grouping of shrubs on the lawn, they heard someone coming along the shadowy gravel path.

A tall man dressed in a flowing black cloak appeared. Since his back was turned to them, he did not notice the couple.

The man, who was unmasked, paused to examine a rose trellis which extended from the ground to the second story of the house. He put his left foot on it and reached up with his right arm.

"What's he up to?" Ned muttered.

The masquerader must have heard the question, for he stepped down quickly. Even then, Ned and Nancy did not see his face. Abruptly the man turned and hastened back into the house.

"Ned, do you suppose he intended to climb the trellis to the library?" Nancy asked.

"It would make a handy ladder." Ned strode over to inspect it.

At the base he picked up a black velvet, hood-type mask. Ned thought that the man in the black cloak might have dropped it.

"Since you can't find your mask, Nancy, try this one for size," he suggested.

Normally, Nancy would not have done so. But she suspected that she might be on the trail of one of the mysterious party thieves!

"I'll wear the hood until we see the man in the black cloak," she agreed.

Returning to the ballroom, she and Ned found the floor even more crowded. In vain, Nancy looked about for the mysterious stranger. Then, unexpectedly, he cut in on Ned!

But now he wore a mask exactly like the one Nancy had on! Before Ned could recover from his surprise, the stranger danced off with Nancy.

"I had a hard time finding you in this crowd," he scolded irritably. "Why didn't you wear the Oriental costume you said you would? If it weren't for the mask, I never would have recognized you."

Nancy remained silent, but her heart was thumping. Someone in an Oriental costume must have dropped the mask she was wearing.

"You nearly wrecked our plan, stupid!" the

man went on. "Can't you learn to obey orders?"

The dancer in the black cloak saw Ned approaching to reclaim his partner.

"Here comes that pest again," he muttered. "Get rid of him as soon as you can."

A moment before Ned tapped him on the shoulder, the man thrust a note into Nancy's hand. She managed to hide her astonishment as they danced away, but once beyond the man's view, Nancy paused beside a cluster of palms. Tersely she explained to Ned what had happened.

"I'm sure that man is one of the party thieves. He mistook me for someone who works with him."

She unfolded the message and read it in an undertone. " 'Eastport Trellis Company offers secondhand window sash on cash terms. In case of rain every cloud has a silver lining.' "

"It must be a hoax, Nancy!"

"I don't think so," she replied soberly. "No, Ned, this message is in code. We must decipher it!"

CHAPTER II

A Daring Theft

NANCY and Ned reread the mysterious note several times, trying to figure out its meaning.

"Maybe the word *trellis* refers to the one we saw the man start to climb," Nancy said.

"Yes, and it's on the *east* side of the house," Ned added.

"The man in the black cloak was looking up at the second-floor windows of the library, Ned. Does that suggest anything?"

"A robbery?"

"This note must mean that there are valuables worth plenty of cash for any thief who climbs that trellis."

"How do you interpret the second sentence of the message?" Ned asked. " 'In case of rain every cloud has a silver lining.' "

"In case—silver. The silver miniatures in the glass case!" Nancy exclaimed.

"You've hit it!" Ned cried out. "I'll bet they

intend to pull a job here tonight—at any minute!"

"We'll have to work fast to stop them. Ned, station yourself at the trellis and keep watch. I'll rush up to the library."

"Better notify the police."

"As soon as I can," Nancy assured him. "There's a telephone in the library. I hope the wires haven't been cut."

The two separated. Nancy looked quickly about the ballroom, hoping to see some of her friends, a member of the Hendrick family, or Linda Seeley. But not one person who might have aided her was in sight. Nancy ran swiftly up the circular stairway.

The moment was a critical one. But the lively young detective had always been able to think fast in an emergency.

Nancy's first case had been *The Secret of the Old Clock*. Since then Nancy had helped countless persons and faced many dangers, including her previous adventure, *Mystery at the Ski Jump*.

As Nancy reached the first landing, beyond view of the ballroom, she was stopped short. Confronting her was a feminine masquerader in a glittering Javanese costume.

"Is this the woman who was supposed to be wearing a black velvet hooded mask?" Nancy wondered. Now she had on a black lace mask, probably the one Nancy had lost.

For an instant the two stared at each other. Nancy caught a glimpse of piercing dark eyes and a cruel mouth. Then the lights went out.

At that instant the woman seized Nancy in a strong grasp and thrust a hand over the girl's mouth. Nancy struggled frantically to free herself, while in the ballroom below there were calls and cries of alarm.

The woman tried to rip off Nancy's mask, but instinct told the young detective to hold onto it. Then as suddenly as she had been seized, Nancy was released. The woman raced down the stairs and disappeared into the darkness. Recovering her breath, Nancy removed the mask and groped her way up to the second floor.

Suddenly the lights went on and Nancy hurried along the hall. Before she reached the library, a maid came running from it.

"Help! Police!" she screamed. "The house has been robbed!"

Nancy stopped the frightened girl, advising her to be quiet and not cause a panic on the crowded floor below.

"Quick!" she urged the maid. "Tell me what happened. Did a thief break into the library?"

"Y-yes. A few minutes ago—through the window. I had my back turned. Suddenly a hand was clapped over my mouth. A blindfold was slipped over my eyes, my hands were tied quick as a flash, and I was gagged!"

"How did you get free?"

"I managed to work the rope off my wrists just as the lights went on. But everything's been taken except the wall paintings!"

"The silver miniatures too?"

"Yes, miss—all that could be carried."

"Which way did the thief go?"

"I couldn't say. He went as quietly as a cat."

"It was a man? Not a woman in a Javanese costume?"

"She was the lookout, I think. Before I was grabbed I saw her wandering around."

From the maid's account, Nancy knew that the daring robbery had been well planned. Undoubtedly the masquerader who had seized her on the landing had been stationed there to see that the thief made a successful getaway under cover of darkness.

Though convinced that it was too late to capture any member of the bold gang, Nancy sped downstairs. Reaching the garden, she called Ned's name. His answering shout informed her that he was still on guard at the trellis.

"What happened?" he demanded as she ran up. "I saw the lights go off."

"The house has been robbed!"

"The library?"

"Yes, and the thieves have escaped."

"No one has come down the trellis since I've been here."

"Then the thief got away before you went on guard or he slipped out of the house while the lights were off," Nancy declared, and then added, "What's this?"

She stared at a tiny piece of cloth which had snagged on a protruding nail in the trellis.

"It must have been torn from that man's cloak!" Nancy exclaimed as she removed it. "Ned, it's a good clue. Come on! Let's see if the thief is still here."

Reentering the house, Nancy and Ned looked around, but he was not among the guests, who now had removed their masks. The couple learned that Linda Seeley had summoned the police. The girl was deeply distressed, fearful that the Hendrick family might blame her for what had taken place.

"I was afraid that this very thing would happen!" she moaned. "If only the Hendricks had allowed a closer check of the guests!"

Nancy and Ned instigated a search of both the house and grounds, but as they had expected, no trace was found of the woman in Javanese garb or the man in the black robe. An empty parking space near the entrance to the house indicated that they had probably left by automobile.

The scream of a siren announced the arrival of a police car. Lieutenant Kelly and Detective Ambrose, whom the Drews knew well, inspected the library, affirming that the thief had entered through the second-story window. From information provided by Nancy and the maid, it was obvious that the man had been aided by at least two accomplices inside the house—probably the woman in the Javanese costume and someone in the basement who had turned off the lights.

The police checked the three areas for fingerprints. Afterward they listened attentively when Nancy and Ned told their story and showed the note, the piece of cloth, and the velvet mask. Then Ambrose went off.

Lieutenant Kelly said, "Nancy, we're certainly obliged to you for this evidence. You say that man you danced with had on a mask like this one?"

"Yes. Would you mind letting me borrow it? I'm interested in the case and would like to look the mask over for clues. I'll bring it to headquarters any time you say."

"I'll have to ask the chief about that," Kelly said. "For you he might do it."

The officer went to the telephone and returned a short time later.

"Okay, Nancy," he said. "I'll photograph the mask and you sign for it." He pulled out a notebook and wrote a receipt, which Nancy signed. "The chief says he'll appreciate your help on this case," Kelly added, smiling, "and we'll let you know when we need the mask."

In the meantime his assistant, Detective Ambrose, a brusque young man, had gone to look for Linda Seeley. He brought her to the group.

"You're in charge of this party?" he asked.

"Yes, Officer," Linda replied. "That is, I am in the absence of Mr. Tombar. At the last minute he had other business to attend to, so he asked me to substitute for him."

"We would like you to answer some questions," Detective Ambrose said sternly, "but of course you do not have to do so without first consulting a lawyer."

Linda turned pale. "I'll answer," she said. "I have nothing to hide."

The detective shot rapid-fire questions at the frightened girl. Who was Mr. Tombar? What company had arranged the party? What precautions had been taken to guard the valuables? Why hadn't invitations been checked more carefully?

As the questions became more pointed, Linda answered them hesitantly. Suddenly Ambrose said, "You'd better come along to headquarters."

"You're accusing me of the theft?" Linda gasped. "I had nothing to do with it!"

Bursting into tears, the girl ran to Nancy. "Don't let them take me to jail!" she pleaded.

"I'm sure," said Nancy, "that Miss Seeley did not commit the robbery. Early in the evening she told me she was worried because there were so many more people here than had been invited."

"Is this true, Mrs. Hendrick?" Ambrose asked.

"Yes, it is," the hostess replied. "We were very foolish not to have taken Miss Seeley's advice about asking our guests to show invitations."

Ambrose thought this over, then glanced at Nancy. "If you say this girl is all right, we'll take your word for it," he said.

"Then come along, Linda," Nancy said, linking arms with her. "Ned and I will drive you home."

After they picked up their wraps, Gloria Hendrick walked with them to the front door. She smiled kindly at the distressed girl.

"We know it wasn't your fault, Linda," she said, "but we have suffered a dreadful loss and the party's ruined. Oh, Nancy, I wish you'd work on the case and help us get back our valuable miniatures. Will you?"

"I'll do what I can," Nancy answered.

On the way home Nancy asked Linda if anyone had rented a black cloak from her company.

"I don't think so, although several people at the party did rent costumes from us."

"And masks?"

"Yes, but not like the one you're carrying."

When Nancy reached home she said good night to Ned. He reminded her of the dance to be given by his cousin Helen Tyne on the twenty-eighth.

"I'll be here early to pick you up."

"I'll be ready."

Nancy's father had waited up for her in his

den. When she related the strange events at the party, Mr. Drew frowned.

"Here's the black velvet hood which the police let me borrow," she concluded, handing it to her father. "I have a hunch it may be an important clue."

"How well do you know Linda Seeley?" her father asked.

"Not too well," she admitted. "Linda was in a few of my classes."

"She may find herself in serious trouble," the lawyer said. "The Lightner Entertainment Company is having legal difficulties. Mr. Lightner, the owner, has appealed to me to defend his firm against several threatened lawsuits."

"Who's bringing them?"

"Former customers whose homes were robbed during parties arranged by the company. They're demanding that he settle for the losses not covered by insurance. They've given him a couple of weeks to decide. Mr. Lightner insists he's not liable."

"You'll defend the firm, Dad?"

"I probably will. Before I commit myself, though, I'd like to investigate the company. The trouble is, I'm tied up in an involved real-estate litigation. The case will take me out of town."

"How about appointing me your assistant?" Nancy proposed. "I'd love to work on the mystery until you're free to take over."

"I suspected as much." Her father chuckled. "All right, Nancy. While I'm away, suppose you check on Mr. Lightner, Linda, and the other employees. Find out what you can."

"I'll do that—first thing," Nancy promised.

The Lightner office was situated on a narrow downtown street in River Heights. Early the next morning Nancy walked to it, and on the pretext of returning the Spanish costumes asked to see Mr. Lightner.

He was a short, slightly built man. "What can I do for you?" he inquired nervously. "I trust you found your costumes satisfactory?"

"In every respect, Mr. Lightner. One of your employees, Linda Seeley, selected them."

"Linda is a very capable girl," the proprietor remarked. "She's been here only a few months, but she learns fast. And she has clever ideas."

Nancy glanced around the room. The office walls were decorated with a variety of weird-looking masks. She complimented Mr. Lightner on his unusual collection, then asked thoughtfully, "You have a great many velvet masks, I suppose?"

"Yes. Most of them are kept in the wardrobe rooms. Would you like to see them?"

"Very much."

Mr. Lightner pressed a buzzer, summoning an employee to show Nancy through the wardrobe rooms.

"I wish I had time to take you around myself," Mr. Lightner said regretfully. "I could talk myself hoarse on the subject of masks."

Nancy asked if there was any particular historical significance connected with the wearing of black velvet masks.

"Oh yes," he replied. "Many men wore them during the reign of Louis XIV in France. In that period of terror and political intrigue it wasn't safe for certain persons to appear on the streets except in disguise. Black velvet hoods were worn especially with wide-sleeved dominoes or robes."

"Do you have some of these robes for rent?"

"Yes. John will show them to you."

John Dale proved to be an attractive and amiable guide. When they finished the tour of the wardrobe rooms, Nancy broached the subject of black dominoes. She told of having been at the Hendricks' masquerade and dancing with a stranger who was wearing that type of robe.

"I've been wondering who he is," she said. "Did you happen to rent such a costume?"

"No, I didn't," John replied. "Everyone who came to me wanted something spectacular. Would you like to see our black cloaks? We have several kinds."

"Yes, I would," Nancy replied, trying to stifle her excitement. It was possible that someone else in the firm had rented the costume to the thief!

CHAPTER III

False Discoveries

JOHN Dale showed Nancy a rack of black cloaks, some with attached hoods. He was closing the glass door of the case when Nancy's eyes fastened on a particular robe.

"Wait!" she exclaimed. "May I see that costume a moment?"

The long black cloak, which hung in graceful folds, had a slight tear near the hem. Examining it closely, Nancy noted that a tiny piece of material was missing and a rose thorn was caught in the frayed threads. This cloak must have been worn by the masked man she and Ned had seen at the garden trellis!

"Was this cloak returned here today?"

"I don't know," John replied. "You'll have to ask either the intake clerk or Mr. Lightner."

"I'll see Mr. Lightner," Nancy decided. "I'll be back in a moment."

She could not find Mr. Lightner immediately. Finally she saw him on the street about to get into his car and beckoned to him. He returned with her to the wardrobe room.

John Dale was no longer there, but he came back shortly, saying that Mr. Tombar, the assistant manager, had asked him to go on an errand.

"Now let's see this cloak you say has a hole in it," Mr. Lightner said to Nancy. "The costume never should have been returned to the rack without being repaired."

Twice Nancy looked through the costumes, examining every one. *The telltale cloak was not there!*

Seeing an empty hanger, she asked John, "Did you remove the one I pointed out to you?"

"Why, no," he answered.

"Then someone took it while you were called away. You saw the cloak yourself only a few minutes ago."

"Yes, I did," the man replied.

Mr. Lightner checked with his other employees by telephone, but all denied having seen or removed the costume.

"Mr. Lightner, would you mind telling me who rented the cloak?" Nancy asked.

"Not at all. Every garment has a number. The one that belongs on this hanger is 4579. Come with me and we'll look into the matter."

Records showed that the cloak, a velvet mask,

and accessories had been rented two days earlier to a James Flobear, Route 1, in Brandon, a small town about twenty miles from River Heights.

Mr. Lightner's next remark stunned Nancy. He said that Linda Seeley had handled the transaction. But Linda had said the night before that her company had not rented any black robes!

Summoned by Mr. Lightner, the girl denied any knowledge of the cloak. "I didn't know that costume had been rented," she declared. "Someone else put my initials on the typed slip."

"What!" Mr. Lightner exclaimed.

He was very upset and summoned every employee in the place. They all came except Mr. Tombar, who was busy with a customer. Each denied any knowledge of the entry for the torn cloak or its disappearance.

Mr. Lightner paced the floor. "This is bad—very bad for business," he declared. "This firm is old and has a fine reputation."

To break the tension Nancy asked how the costume had been returned. None of the employees had an answer.

Deeply troubled over the incident, Nancy decided to make an attempt to track down James Flobear. A short time later she left the entertainment company and telephoned the Brandon police. She learned that no one by the name of Flobear lived in or near the town.

"Just as I suspected," Nancy said to herself.

"Obviously a false name was given so there could be no follow-up. And whoever had charge of the transaction at Lightner's is afraid of becoming involved or may even be working with the party thieves!"

Next, Nancy went to police headquarters, where she talked with Chief McGinnis. He praised her for her detective work at the Hendricks' masquerade party, and listened attentively as she reported her new discoveries.

"You have a very keen eye for clues, Nancy," the chief said with a smile. "You certainly beat us to that one. I'll send a man over to Lightner's to check on the cloak episode."

Nancy asked if the police had at any time suspected the entertainment company in connection with the party robberies.

"We, of course, ran a routine check on the company. Had everyone in it shadowed for two weeks, even Mr. Lightner. But we didn't find evidence against any of them."

Nancy said quickly, "Last night Detective Ambrose seemed very suspicious of Linda Seeley who works there."

"We're keeping our eyes on her," the chief admitted. "But there's no direct evidence against her, you understand. It's possible she may be accepting a percentage on each haul for supplying information. Miss Seeley may be working with the gang and also with servants in the homes where big parties are arranged by the Lightner Entertainment Company.

"The girl has a clean record so far," the captain continued. "We never would have suspected her if we hadn't been tipped off by her boss."

"Mr. Lightner?" Nancy gasped.

"No, by his assistant, Peter Tombar. He suggested that the girl might bear watching, because she was specifically in charge of certain parties at which robberies took place."

"I just can't believe Linda is guilty," Nancy said.

She left police headquarters more troubled than ever over the girl's predicament. Could Peter Tombar's opinion be trusted?

"I think I'll go and have a talk with him," she reflected.

It was nearing noontime when she reached the Lightner offices. Most of the employees had gone to lunch, but Mr. Tombar was there. A secretary directed Nancy to a rear room where he was inspecting an Egyptian mask.

Peter Tombar cast an unfriendly glance at Nancy. He was a rather stout man, dark-complexioned, with a hard, determined set to his jaw.

Nancy sensed instantly that Mr. Tombar would not cooperate unless it suited his purpose to answer her questions. Lowering her voice and assuming a confidential manner, she introduced herself as a private investigator.

"Mr. Tombar, I'm here to check up on one of your employees—a girl named Linda Seeley."

A glint of satisfaction flickered in the man's dark eyes. Immediately he became less guarded.

"In trouble with the police, isn't she?" he demanded. "I told Mr. Lightner a week ago that that girl would get the company in hot water."

"Tell me what you know about her," Nancy urged.

"She's flighty. Scatterbrained, I'd call her."

"You've caught her in mistakes?"

"Well, not exactly," Tombar admitted reluctantly. "She's crafty. Twists like a pretzel when you try to pin her down."

"Then you actually haven't anything against her?" Nancy continued.

"A man has his own reasons for not liking hired help and he doesn't have to tell why!"

Nancy decided not to pursue this line of questioning and asked calmly, "By the way, have you any theory concerning the recent party thefts?"

"I have!" Tombar returned with emphasis. "And I guess you know the person I mean."

Nancy nodded. But more convinced than ever of Linda's innocence, she felt an even stronger urge to help the girl. Tombar plainly intended to have Linda discharged if he could find some pretext.

Nancy left his office and walked across the street. Her dislike of the man was increasing and she wondered what motive he had for casting suspicion on Linda.

Passing a drugstore with a soda counter, Nancy went in for a sandwich. To her delight Linda was there too. She slid onto a stool beside her.

After giving her order, she drew Linda into conversation. The girl seemed very despondent, and Nancy could guess the reason.

"It's Mr. Tombar," Linda confessed. "He lectured me again this morning."

"What about?"

"The robbery last night, and the missing black cloak."

"The cloak hasn't been found?"

"Not yet. Mr. Lightner is most annoyed. Oh, everyone's in a frightful mood."

As Nancy stirred her iced tea, she said, "Tell me about Mr. Tombar. What's he like?"

"Vinegar and acid. He's efficient, though. Mr. Lightner depends on him, but Mr. Tombar's a slave driver, always bawling out employees if they're a minute late."

"Is he always on time himself?" Nancy asked.

"Oh yes. But he makes up for it by taking a two-hour lunch nearly every day. He waits until the others get back, then goes off alone."

"Where does he eat?" Nancy asked.

"I don't know," Linda answered. "Maybe out of town. He always takes his car."

Two hours for lunch was a long time for a

strict disciplinarian like Tombar! The information interested Nancy, who mulled over it as she ate her sandwich.

"I must go now," Linda said with an anxious glance at the wall clock. "See you later."

Alone, Nancy leisurely finished her lunch. As she left the drugstore, she chanced to look across the street toward the Lightner offices.

Peter Tombar was just coming out, a package in his hand. Nancy saw him walk briskly to a green sedan parked a short distance away. A wild thought came to her. Did he have the torn cloak with him?

Nancy noted that not only the wheels but the fenders were heavily caked with mud. Evidently Tombar had driven recently on unpaved roads in the country. He might be going there now to dispose of the black robe!

Nancy wished she had driven her own car downtown that morning, but the crisp, cool breeze had encouraged her to walk. Just then a taxi rounded the corner. Instantly Nancy hailed the driver and hopped in.

"Follow that green car ahead!" she directed as Tombar pulled out.

"Friend of yours?" The taximan grinned.

"No, just the opposite," Nancy replied.

"Okay, lady. Here goes!"

Nancy feared that Peter Tombar might have seen her action and give the cab a merry chase.

Her fears were well-founded. The green sedan raced to the first corner and turned right. Seconds before the taxi reached the intersection, the traffic light turned red! The sedan carrying Peter Tombar and perhaps the missing cloak was far down the side street.

"That old boy's sure stepping on it," the driver declared. "You want me to try keeping him in sight?"

"I certainly do."

"Then sit tight, miss," he directed.

The light changed again and the taxi shot ahead.

"Look back and see if any cops are coming," the driver said.

"Okay," Nancy agreed, thinking perhaps she might need them.

CHAPTER IV

Confusion

THE Tombar car raced through a stoplight, skidding around a second corner.

"That fellow's a lunatic!" Nancy's taxi driver muttered.

"Take it a little slower," she advised nervously. "It's not worth a smash-up."

As she spoke, they heard the shrill scream of brakes ahead. At a busy intersection, Tombar had sped through another red light. Oncoming traffic had halted barely in time to prevent a collision.

Unmindful, Tombar raced on. Nancy watched as he turned left at the first side street beyond the intersection.

Again the taxi driver was forced to wait for a traffic light to change. When he finally reached the side street, the green sedan had vanished.

"Never mind. It's no use trying to pick up the trail now," Nancy told the driver after they had cruised around two blocks without seeing Tombar's car. "He knew we were following him."

"He sure tried hard to shake us," the taximan agreed.

Nancy told the driver to take her home and tipped him generously for the brief but speedy ride. She was convinced that Peter Tombar did not want her to know where he was going. She decided his movements would bear watching.

The following day Nancy went to the Lightner building and waited outside for Linda until she finished work. Nancy offered the girl a ride home, and during the drive asked her if she knew what Tombar had in the package he had taken away the previous noon. Linda said she had no idea, but that he was always carrying packages of one sort or another.

"In connection with his work?"

"I imagine so," was Linda's vague response.

Nancy inquired whether Lightner Entertainment Company had any big parties scheduled in the near future.

"Our business has fallen off a lot lately since the robberies have received so much publicity. There's the Becker wedding, though, Tuesday night, at their home."

"The Beckers are prominent socially," Nancy mused. "There will be a room full of expensive wedding presents. Just the sort of setup to tempt a thief."

"Don't suggest such a thing," Linda replied with a shiver. "One more robbery and our company may be ruined."

"Then why not take special precautions?"

"Oh, we have! Mr. Tombar has arranged for plainclothesmen to watch the guests. As an added safety measure, Mr. Lightner suggested that a reliable servant be assigned to guard the silver. Mr. Tombar thought that entirely unnecessary, but he was overruled."

"Even so, there could be a slip-up," Nancy insisted. "Those thieves are clever."

"How well I know! I wish you were going to be there! You caught a glimpse of the thieves at Gloria's party and might recognize them if they dare to appear again."

Nancy agreed, quickly seizing upon the suggestion. "Can you get me an invitation?"

"No, but Mr. Lightner could," said Linda, "and I'm sure he'd be glad to do it. He's very eager to have the thieves caught. I'll call him about it tonight."

"Thanks a lot," said Nancy. "Will you try to arrange it so that I can arrive early? I want to look over the house before any guests come."

"That shouldn't be hard," Linda replied. "Oh, Nancy, if you can prevent a robbery, Lightner's will be so grateful!" Suddenly she frowned. "I'm afraid Mr. Tombar won't like your being there. He hates to have anyone change his plans. But don't worry," she added quickly. "I feel sure Mr. Lightner will approve."

Linda kept her promise and the next day Nancy received a note from Mrs. Becker. Tuesday evening Nancy dressed and drove to the luxurious Becker home. She was met at the door by a pleasant butler.

"Your invitation, please, miss," he requested. Nancy showed him the note.

"Miss Seeley told us we might expect you," the butler said. "Come in, please."

The Becker home had been beautifully decorated with palms and flowers screening every corner of the spacious house. Nancy reflected that they would offer perfect protection for any uninvited guest!

Wandering around the first floor, she noticed that men had been stationed at all outside doors. She was brought up short as she came face to face with Detective Ambrose.

"You here as a guest or to help us?" he asked brusquely.

Nancy laughed. "Perhaps both."

"Well, you may be sorry you showed up. I'm afraid there'll be trouble."

"You mean the party thieves might be here?"

The detective straightened himself up confidently and replied, "I happen to know we should be on the lookout for a crook who'll try to pass himself off as a highbrow Englishman."

Nancy wondered from whom Detective Ambrose had received the tip. She did not wish to encourage his seeming arrogance, however, and said assuredly, "I'll keep an eye out for him."

Nancy moved away. Continuing her tour of the ground floor, she noted the location of various treasures.

"But I doubt that a thief would try to steal anything from the first floor," she reasoned. "It's too well guarded."

Learning from Linda Seeley, whom she met in the hall, that the wedding presents were displayed on the second floor, Nancy went upstairs. The gifts had been attractively arranged on long tables in a narrow room lined with mirrors.

Although Nancy had attended many fine weddings, this array of silver and crystal took her breath away. "They're magnificent!" she thought.

The only guard in evidence was an elderly servant. Beside him was a house telephone.

"Are you alone here?" Nancy asked.

"Yes, miss," he responded. "Mrs. Becker instructed me not to leave this room until the reception is over and the last guest gone."

Nancy supposed that the old man was a trusted and faithful servant. Nevertheless, it seemed to her that it would have been far wiser to have assigned a policeman to the upper floor.

She decided to ask Detective Ambrose about it. Nancy could not find him, for the bridal party had just returned from the church. Photographers flocked about them taking pictures and guests were arriving in large numbers.

Hearing a slight commotion at the front entrance, Nancy turned in that direction. Detective Ambrose was questioning a tall, white-mustached man. As she came closer, Nancy heard him speak with a pronounced English accent!

"But I mislaid the invitation," he said crisply.

Nancy guessed what had occurred. Since the man had appeared without an invitation, the butler had summoned Detective Ambrose.

The newcomer, indignant at being denied entrance, tapped his cane impatiently. "Dashed if I can understand all this fuss about an invitation. I have explained to the butler that I was detained at my hotel by Lord Atchfield. Hence the invitation was forgotten. Let me pass."

"Don't be in such a rush," Detective Ambrose advised him sharply. "Your getup and your speech don't fool me."

"My getup? I say, your words mystify me. Mrs. Becker certainly shall hear of this affront!"

"You bet she will!" Detective Ambrose replied firmly. "Come along. If a member of the family can identify you, fine. Otherwise, you're going with me to headquarters."

"Police headquarters! I say, old chap, you're making a frightful mistake."

Despite the Englishman's protests, the detective ushered him inside. He asked the butler to bring Mr. Becker to the hall. In a moment the worried father of the bride stepped out of the receiving line.

"This man's trying to get in without an invitation," the detective informed him. "Says his name is Earl Contrey."

"The Earl of Contrey, Sussex," the guest corrected, bowing slightly. "Sorry to have caused all this trouble, but—"

"I never saw this man before," broke in Mr. Becker.

"Ha!" chortled Detective Ambrose. He gripped the Englishman's arm. "Just as I thought! I figured that brush of yours was a fake!" he added.

"I say!" the guest sputtered. "My mustache and I are quite real. I demand that you notify Mrs. Becker of my presence immediately."

The bride's father had already turned away.

"Okay, pal," Ambrose said. "Let's just say you've been grooming your act for a long time. Come along peaceful-like or I'll put handcuffs on you."

Nancy vaguely recalled having read in the newspaper a few days previously of the arrival in New York of the Earl of Contrey. Suppose this man were he and not the thief in disguise!

Determined to check the matter herself, she quickly approached the receiving line and whispered to the bride's mother.

"Do you know the Earl of Contrey?"

"Indeed I do!" exclaimed Mrs. Becker. "He's an old friend of mine. Don't tell me he flew from New York to attend our daughter's reception!"

Mr. Becker was horrified at the turn of events. Quickly his wife explained that she had read of the Earl's arrival and had sent him a last-minute invitation.

Together she and her husband followed Nancy to where the detective's car was parked. Mrs. Becker shook the Earl's hand as her husband greeted him and apologized profusely for what had happened.

"We have this young lady to thank," Mrs. Becker said, turning to Nancy. "I presume you're helping the Lightner people?"

"Yes, Mrs. Becker," she replied.

Detective Ambrose glared at Nancy. Then he muttered, "I was only trying to do my duty, ma'am. We were tipped off to watch for an Englishman, and this guy—I mean the Earl—fit the bill. Your husband couldn't identify him."

"Of course not. They've never met. I hope you make no further mistakes of this nature."

Suddenly Nancy realized that if the thief and his accomplices had been waiting for a chance to get into the house without showing invitations, they had had a golden opportunity. Both the detective and the butler had been away from the front door for several minutes and the elderly servant had been left alone to guard the valuable presents!

Worried, Nancy returned to the house and hastened to the second floor. The door to the room in which the wedding gifts were displayed now was closed. She gently twisted the knob and was startled to discover that the door was locked.

"Perhaps one of the plainclothesmen locked the door when the trouble started," she said to herself, trying not to think the worst.

Nancy noticed that a door to an adjoining bedroom stood ajar. She peered inside. Seeing no one there, she tiptoed in.

A velvet curtain screened the entranceway into the locked room. Moving noiselessly to the heavy drapery, Nancy cautiously parted it and stepped inside.

Involuntarily she drew back at the sight before her. The elderly servant lay sprawled on the floor, apparently unconscious.

In front of a table on which silver pieces were displayed stood a man in formal summer attire with gloves. He wore a velvet hooded mask over his head! The thief was putting the wedding gifts into a dark cloth, drawstring bag.

"I must get help!" Nancy thought. She glanced at the nearby telephone.

The thief, sensing he was being watched, whirled. "So it's the great girl detective!" he hissed at Nancy.

His voice was that of the brusque man who had danced with her at the Hendricks' masquerade! The one who had mistaken her for an assistant of his!

He yanked the long cord from the bag and stretched it taut between his fingers. Nancy stiffened as he stepped menacingly toward her.

CHAPTER V

Strange Numbers

INSTANTLY Nancy seized the house telephone and pushed the signal button. "Help!" she screamed into the mouthpiece.

To her amazement, the thief flung himself away from her and jumped across one of the tables. He opened a mirrored door in the wall and fled, banging it after him.

Still shouting for help, Nancy pursued him. The man evidently knew every inch of the rambling house. He ran along a back hall, through a door, and directly to the servants' stairway.

Nancy followed him down the stairs, crying, "Stop, thief!"

Reaching the foot of the stairs, she found he had locked the door. Nancy pounded on it and presently the door was opened by a startled maid. In a moment the place was in an uproar with everyone trying to locate the fugitive. No one had seen him come through the stairway door.

The shouts had attracted Detective Ambrose and the other plainclothesmen. At once they made a search for the thief. Nancy listened to the voice of every man wearing summer formals, hoping to discover the one who had spoken to her upstairs. But apparently the thief had escaped.

"Maybe I can learn something from that old servant," Nancy said to herself.

She went upstairs and found that her first cry of help on the telephone had brought a maid to aid the elderly man. By now he had revived and was seated in a chair in the bedroom.

"I don't know how it happened," he said. "I never even saw the person who hit me. He sneaked up from behind."

Detective Ambrose came in at that moment. He reported no success in apprehending the would-be thief.

"At least he didn't get away with anything this time," the officer remarked. "Our quick work saved the wedding silver."

"Yes, we were lucky," Nancy replied, smiling at the detective's use of the word *our*.

Since the servant guard could offer no clues, she returned to the reception. The gaiety which had prevailed half an hour earlier was gone from the party.

Nancy remained awhile, departing when the

bride left. At home she was surprised to find Bess Marvin and George Fayne. They explained that they had come, hoping to hear about her experiences at the reception.

Nancy laughed. "Who said I had any?"

"Why, it's written all over your face," George declared. "Come on. Tell us. Did you have another encounter with the man in the mask?"

"I did," Nancy said, and went on to relate how the thief had eluded her.

"Wish I'd been there," George remarked, her eyes dancing. "I'd have helped you hold him, Nancy."

"I could have used a little of your muscle, George. He's a slippery rascal!"

"Aren't you afraid he'll try to get even with you?" Bess asked nervously. "After all, you wrecked his plans tonight, Nancy, and he won't forget that."

"I'm not worried."

"You and Mrs. Gruen will be in the house alone tonight, won't you?"

"Yes, Dad is still away on a trip. I'm not the least bit afraid, though."

At that moment the telephone rang. In the quiet house the sound was startling.

"It's probably Dad calling long distance," Nancy said. "I've been expecting him to phone."

Excusing herself, she went to the hall and picked up the telephone. At first there was no reply to her hello. Then a man's voice spoke precisely and with a sinister inflection:

"Nancy Drew, keep out of affairs that aren't your own! If you don't, be prepared to pay the consequences. Another warning. Get rid of that hooded mask. Drop it within twenty-four hours over the wall of Hillside Cemetery."

The receiver clicked, indicating the end of the one-way conversation. Bess and George had joined her, aware that something was amiss.

"Was it a threat?" George demanded.

Nancy nodded. "I've been ordered to get rid of the black mask I picked up at Gloria's home."

"Oh, Nancy!" Bess exclaimed. "Didn't I tell you? Why did you ever keep the mask?"

"I intend to hold on to it until the police ask me for it."

"Good for you, Nancy!" George approved. "Don't let that man bluff you!"

Bess sighed. "Well, if you're not afraid, I guess we may as well run along. It's getting late. But do be careful, Nancy."

After the girls had gone, Nancy locked the screen door, but left the front door open, for the night was very warm.

She sat for a while in the living room, thinking about the new developments in the case. Then, abruptly, she went to a desk drawer and took out the black hooded mask.

As she was gazing at it, Mrs. Gruen came downstairs from her room.

"Nancy, I think you should go to bed," she remarked. Then noticing the mask in the girl's hand, she added with a shudder, "Mooning over that sinister thing again?"

"It's my most valuable clue! This might be the very thing I need to track down the thieves."

Nancy revealed to the housekeeper that she had been ordered to get rid of the mask.

"Well, obey their orders. I heard you telling Bess and George about your adventure tonight. The whole thing sounds dangerous to me."

"Now, Hannah, don't get so upset. Please. You know when I'm caught in a tight spot I can usually manage to get out of it."

"Just you wait, Nancy Drew. Someday you won't be able to find a way out. I worry all the time about you and your father. Two of a kind!"

"Well, then," Nancy replied, "there's no need to worry if I'm like Dad. He has never failed to crack a tough case!"

The housekeeper realized that it was futile to urge Nancy to stop work on a mystery, once she had started.

"What is it now, Nancy? Why are you staring so hard at that mask?" Hannah asked.

"It just occurred to me," Nancy replied, "that the thief must have a good reason why he wants this returned. Perhaps it contains some clue he doesn't want me to find."

While Mrs. Gruen watched, Nancy ripped out the white silk lining of the velvet mask. To her disappointment, nothing had been hidden inside.

"I guess I was wrong," she admitted ruefully. "I thought jewels or something valuable might have been tucked under the padding."

"I'll sew the lining back in," the housekeeper offered. "Not tonight, though. I'm too sleepy."

As Nancy started to tuck the lining back in, she noticed some numbers written on the reverse side.

"What's this?" she said.

Carrying it to a brighter light, Nancy studied the numbers. They read: 621 626 628 71 75.

"What do they mean?" Mrs. Gruen asked.

"I wish I knew," Nancy replied.

"The ink appears fairly fresh," Mrs. Gruen remarked. "Not faded as it would be if the cloth were old."

"The numbers may be a code. I wonder—"

At that moment the telephone rang and Nancy hastened to answer it. This time it was her father.

"I'm so glad to hear from you. How's everything?" Nancy asked cheerily.

"Fine on this end. How about you?"

She reported what she had been doing on the case, then told him of the numbers on the mask's lining.

"The numbers may be a code," Nancy said

"Read them to me," Mr. Drew suggested.

After Nancy did so, he said, "Very interesting. They sound like dates."

"You mean 621 is June twenty-first?"

"Yes. And the last one's the day after the Fourth of July."

"Oh, Dad, you're wonderful! That's probably exactly what they are—dates for planned thefts! The woman in the Javanese costume put them in, or someone wrote them down before giving her the mask so she wouldn't forget them."

"Nancy, here's a suggestion. Call the Lightner Entertainment Company in the morning and find out if they coincide with parties they're arranging. But be discreet in asking questions."

"I will!" Nancy assured him. "And Dad, when are you coming home?"

Mr. Drew said that unless something unexpected came up he would return the following evening.

"We miss you," she said. "By the way, you're at the Excelsior in Amstar, aren't you?"

As Nancy said good-by she heard a sound on the front porch. Thinking someone was arriving, she went to look out, but no one was there.

"My imagination, I guess," she decided. She closed and locked the front door, then went up to bed.

Nancy telephoned Linda Seeley at nine o'clock the following morning. After explaining where she had obtained the dates, she asked if Lightner's had any parties scheduled for them.

"Yes, we do have for the first three you mentioned," Linda answered without hesitation. "I know, because I've worked on them myself. Wait, I'll check the others."

In a moment she returned to say that July first was on their books, but the office had no record of a party for the fifth.

"I'll contact the social editor of the newspaper," Nancy said. "Someone may be giving a big party without Lightner's services."

"Nancy, if you're still working on the theft, you'd better be wary," Linda advised hurriedly. "After what happened last night at the reception, I'm getting scared."

Nancy wanted to ask more questions, but Linda suddenly warned her that she must end the conversation.

"Mr. Tombar is coming!" she said nervously. "I'll get in touch with you later."

"Just one thing," Nancy interposed. "Has a masquerade party been scheduled for any of those dates I told you about?"

"No, only other types of parties," Linda whispered. "Good-by!"

Nancy next called the newspaper. The social editor, a friend, said she knew of no large parties scheduled for July fifth. "If I hear of any, Nancy, I'll call you."

Nancy thanked her. Putting down the phone, she sat still, absorbed in thought. Her reflections were interrupted by the excited barking of Togo, her small terrier. He had jumped up on his hind legs and was scratching at a window sill.

"Togo, what's wrong?" Nancy demanded.

Mrs. Gruen had gone to the window and was peering into the sunny side yard. Nancy joined her. No one was in sight.

"Togo, you were really fooled this time," Nancy scolded him. "No one's out there."

The little terrier, however, continued to bark. He ran to the front door, jerking his head and scratching frantically with his paws to tell Nancy that he wanted to be let out.

"What can be the matter?" she said, frowning. "I've never seen him so persistent."

She ordered the dog to come away from the door and lie down. To her vexation, the usually obedient Togo paid no attention to her command. She started toward him, but whirled around at a sharp exclamation from Hannah.

"There *was* someone lurking near the window!" the housekeeper whispered. "Nancy, I just saw a long shadow move across the porch."

Nancy dashed for the door, recalling the sound she had heard the night before.

"Someone's eavesdropping on us!" she exclaimed.

CHAPTER VI

Kidnapped!

As Nancy opened the door, Togo bounded outside. The little dog raced directly toward the garage, barking furiously.

"He saw someone, all right," Nancy declared. She could see the vague impressions of a man's footprints leading directly to the window near the telephone. "Someone was listening. I'm going to look around outside."

She asked the housekeeper to watch from the window while she followed the dog to the garage. The building was empty.

Togo ran around the yard, his nose to the ground. Picking up the stranger's scent, he followed it to the street but became confused.

"Whoever it was, he's gone now, Togo," Nancy said, calling him back into the house. "Good dog! You tried hard."

The housekeeper was greatly upset by the disturbance.

"Probably it was a member of that Velvet Gang," she remarked. "That's what the newspaper called them. I suspect the man wanted to get his black hood."

"Now stop worrying," Nancy begged. "If he'd wanted it, he would have tried harder to get in. Nevertheless I'll phone Chief McGinnis."

She brought the officer up to date on all she had learned and asked if she might still retain the mask since her father wanted to see it again.

"All right," the chief said. "So long as we have those dates, that's the important thing."

Mrs. Gruen remained jumpy and Nancy did not leave her. Hours later, when she and Nancy went upstairs, the housekeeper gave a sudden start.

"Listen!" she said tensely. "What was that?"

"Only the front doorbell. I'll go."

"Be careful, Nancy. It may be a trick."

The housekeeper's suspicions were unwarranted. Opening the door, Nancy found a messenger from the telegraph office. She took the envelope which was addressed to her and tore it open. The telegram read:

AMSTAR

HAVE FOUND WHAT DATES MEAN. COME MY HOTEL THIS EVENING. BRING MASK.

It was signed "Dad."

"Bad news?" Mrs. Gruen asked, hovering near.

"Not exactly." Nancy was rereading the telegram. "This message has me puzzled, though. Why should Dad ask me to come to Amstar when he expects to arrive home tonight?"

She offered the telegram to Mrs. Gruen for her opinion.

"Apparently your father has some further information on the mystery," she said after reading it.

"This telegram may be a hoax."

"That's possible," Mrs. Gruen admitted. "Well, the only thing to do is to verify it."

Nancy put in a long-distance call to her father. The hotel operator informed her that Carson Drew was not in his room. She assured the girl, however, that he had not checked out.

Turning from the telephone, Nancy said reassuringly to worried Mrs. Gruen:

"Evidently Dad sent the telegram, so I'd better take the mask and meet him."

She got in touch with the railroad station and learned that the only through train to Amstar left in less than two hours.

"Since Dad wants me there this evening, I'll have to take it," she remarked.

As she spoke, Togo growled and ran to the door.

"Another eavesdropper!" Hannah Gruen cried. She followed as Nancy ran outside.

A man was dashing across the lawn. He jumped

into a car parked in front of the house next door.

"There he goes!" Nancy said grimly as the automobile roared off. Sensing the housekeeper's nervousness, she added, "Perhaps Bess and George should stay with you tonight. I'll call them." She phoned George and asked her to pick up Bess.

"Be there in fifteen minutes," George promised.

While Hannah Gruen hurriedly pressed a suit for Nancy, the girl detective started packing her overnight suitcase.

"I mustn't forget to take the black mask," she told herself.

When Bess and George arrived, they were astonished to learn that she was leaving at once for Amstar.

"Nancy, you're not going alone!" Bess protested. "George and I will make the trip with you. Why, someone might try to snatch that mask away if you're alone."

George snapped her fingers. "That gives me an idea. It will make your trip mugging-proof."

"What's your idea?" Nancy asked eagerly.

"I'll masquerade as you! I can wear your clothes and carry your bag."

"That's a very dangerous idea. I don't think—"

"I insist. After all, it's the most foolproof way I can think of to protect River Heights' number one detective," George interrupted. She fluffed her hair and added, "We'll rent a titian-haired wig for me and a dark-brown one for you."

Nancy was thoughtful. Although she worried about her friend's welfare, the idea appealed to her. If the girls' hunches were right, she might even catch the person who wanted the mask back!

"Well, what say?" George prodded.

"There's one drawback," said Nancy. "With eavesdroppers around I don't think any of us should rent the wigs."

"That problem can be solved easily." George looked over Nancy's shoulder. "Here's the person to do it. Hello, Mrs. Gruen."

"What am I getting into?" the housekeeper asked with a smile.

While Nancy explained, George went to the phone and called Mrs. Fayne and Mrs. Marvin who gave their permission for the trip. Ten minutes later Mrs. Gruen was in a taxi on her way to the Lightner Entertainment Company.

Meanwhile, it was decided that the mask would be carried in Bess's bag. As soon as Mrs. Gruen returned with the wigs and the train tickets, George took Nancy's initialed suitcase and the cousins left to return home to dress for the trip.

"Hurry! There's not much time!" Nancy called to them. "And, Bess, take a bag without initials. I will too."

"I'm glad they're going with you," Hannah declared. "You'll need protection more than I will."

Bess and Nancy met on the station platform just as the train arrived.

By prearrangement they took seats near the rear of the second coach. Soon George came in with her luggage. Seating herself at the front of the car, she set the case so that the initials N.D. were plainly visible to anyone passing through the aisle.

"I hope the trick works," Bess whispered.

"It will," Nancy predicted, although both girls remained silently concerned for George's safety.

Nancy nudged Bess to draw her attention to three passengers who had entered the car directly behind George. One was a dark-eyed, sullen-looking woman in smartly tailored clothes. She was accompanied by two men.

They scrutinized George, who was thumbing through a magazine. Then their gaze wandered down the aisle to Nancy and Bess.

The woman and one of the men sat down in the double seat across the aisle from George. The second man took the seat directly in front of Bess and Nancy.

This was an unforeseen complication, for now they were unable to talk without fear of being overheard. Nevertheless, Nancy and Bess were jubilant. They were certain their ruse had worked!

The three passengers easily might have chosen other seats. Instead, two had deliberately sat near

the girl they thought was Nancy, and the third
had probably stationed himself to listen to Nancy
and Bess, the only other two young women in
the car.

Nancy settled back in her seat and opened a
magazine but did not read. The man in the seat
ahead paid no attention to the other passengers
and devoted himself to a copy of a New York
newspaper.

An hour later the conductor called out the
name of a small but busy town. Nancy noticed
that the stranger had put aside his newspaper.
Was he going to leave the train? Had she been
entirely mistaken about him?

Nancy and Bess did not venture even a whispered remark. But they exchanged glances.

The train began to slow down for the station.
Nancy and Bess looked up to see what the couple
across the aisle from George would do.

The dark-haired woman rose, stepped across
the aisle, and bent over George. When she
straightened, the masquerading "Nancy Drew"
had slumped over, apparently in a faint!

"Oh dear! Our daughter is ill," the woman
proclaimed in a loud voice. "We must get her off
the train at once!"

By this time they had reached the station. The
woman seized the suitcase with the initials N.D.
Her companion gathered George up in his arms,
carrying her toward the front exit.

Alarmed, Nancy and Bess grabbed their bags and started in pursuit. But their way was immediately blocked by the man who had seated himself directly ahead of them.

"What's the hurry, sister?" he asked, swaying from side to side to prevent their pushing past him.

Nancy knew now why he had taken that particular seat. George's kidnapping had been planned —her abductors wanted no interference!

"Let us through!" Nancy ordered.

"There's plenty of time, girlie."

"No, there isn't," Bess fairly yelled.

By now several other passengers began to take an interest in the commotion.

"The rear exit!" Nancy whispered.

She wheeled and Bess followed her. They leaped down the steps, and looking up the platform, saw the unconscious George being put into a waiting automobile. As Nancy and Bess dropped their bags and ran toward it, the car sped away from the station!

CHAPTER VII

Double Talk

"STOP! Stop that car!" Bess cried frantically. "They're kidnapping George!"

"It's no use," said Nancy, seizing her friend's arm. "I'll go look for a policeman. Now brace up, Bess," she added sternly. "Try to find the man who stopped us."

As Nancy raced off, Bess bit her trembling lip and turned back. She spotted the man; but, to her dismay, he was driving away, in a different direction from the one which the kidnappers' car had taken.

In the meantime George was slowly regaining consciousness. But she could not move a single muscle, not even those of her eyelids. As if from a great distance she heard a man say:

"Well done. This time Nancy Drew wasn't so smart. You got the mask?"

"It should be in her suitcase," a woman's voice informed him.

"Then dig it out fast! We haven't got all day, you know. It has to be burned before this girl comes to. Then we'll make her talk."

"The whiff I gave her will easily last that long," the woman said.

George could hear her opening the locks on the suitcase.

"Something's wrong," the woman muttered. "It's not here."

"What!" the man thundered.

"Look at this blouse with the initials G.F. This girl isn't Nancy Drew!"

"Idiot!" another man stormed. "Are you sure?"

"But we thought from the suitcase and her hair—"

"You thought!" the man mocked her. "I'll take a look at the girl myself."

He pulled the car into a clearing at the side of the road. Alighting, the driver opened the back door and stared at the seemingly sleeping George.

"She's a phony! Look! She's wearing a wig!" he cried, snatching it off.

"You've been outwitted, and by Nancy Drew!" the other man yelled. "No telling what she's done about those dates in the mask by this time. Now we're really in a spot. And this girl's coming around," he observed as George stirred. "She'll be a nuisance to us. Blindfold her!"

George tried to open her eyes but she could not do it, her eyelids felt so heavy. A handkerchief was bound tightly across her eyes. She realized her danger, but even this thought failed to rouse her from the stupor into which she had fallen.

"Where is the black velvet hood?" the woman hissed in her ear. "What did Nancy Drew do with it?"

There was no answer. Even if George had wanted to, she would have been unable to respond. Her mind was so befogged at the moment that the woman's question was a meaningless jumble of words.

"Talk!" ordered the driver.

But George was overcome with drowsiness and a new sensation of numbness spread through her limbs.

"You gave her too big a dose," the other man accused the woman. "Can't you see she's going under again?"

"Yeah," broke in the driver. "A lot of good she'll do us now!"

"Okay, okay," growled the woman. "So I gave her too much. We'd just better get out of here fast before the Drew girl puts the cops on us."

"Listen! A car's coming!" said the driver. "Let's get rid of this babe and scram!"

Hastily George's captors pulled her from the automobile and propped her beside a tree, together with her own handbag and Nancy's suit-case.

"Now, young lady, how do you like that?" the woman sneered.

She grasped George's arm tightly, whispering dire threats into her ear. Although George was dazed, the words burned deeply into her brain.

"And I advise you not to forget!" the woman finished with a harsh laugh.

"Come on! Hurry!" the driver shouted.

The couple jumped back into the car and roared away in a cloud of dust. George gave a sigh and sank to the foot of the tree in a deep sleep.

Meanwhile Bess had found Nancy, who was relating their story to a policeman. When she finished, Bess told about the escape of the other man.

"Did you get the license number of the kid-nappers' car?" the officer asked.

Both shook their heads. "Everything happened so quickly. I didn't see the other one either," Bess apologized, then broke off in sobs.

"The kidnappers had a brown sedan," Nancy recalled. "It turned right at the first corner. Can you chase it?"

"I can't leave here, but I'll report it," the policeman said. "Did you notice anything else?"

"No-o," Nancy replied. "That is, nothing that will help us now."

Actually she had made one other fleeting observation. Just as the car crossed the railroad tracks, she had seen a small object drop out of a window. From a distance it had looked like a shiny metal disk. Nancy wanted to search for it, but just now there was no time, and moreover another train was arriving.

"If the kidnappers took Old Mill Road, it's a case for the State Police," the officer said. "I'll call them."

The girls ran back to the platform for their bags but returned at once. They waited impatiently. Finally the officer appeared.

"Okay, they'll try to pick up the trail," he reported, "but they'd like you girls along."

"Where do we meet them?" Nancy asked, fidgety that time was passing and George was getting farther away.

"Their headquarters are on Old Mill Road. I'll take you there."

The girls picked up their overnight bags and jumped into his car, which sped to the outskirts of town. There was no sign of the brown sedan.

They transferred to a waiting State Police car containing two officers who introduced themselves as Lieutenants Connolly and Whyte.

They recognized Nancy from newspaper pictures which had often accompanied stories of her detective work. Nancy thanked them for their praise but quickly turned their attention to the details of George's abduction.

"The Velvet Gang, eh?" Whyte said. "This is serious."

The four kept a sharp lookout for the kidnappers' car. There was no way of knowing whether or not they had taken the right route as they followed the winding Old Mill Road.

Presently Whyte radioed to headquarters, reporting failure so far and asking if there was any news from surrounding towns which had been alerted. He was told that the abductors had not been picked up.

The officer had just replaced his transceiver when Nancy cried out, "Stop! Look over there!"

Her alert eyes had caught sight of a girl propped against a tree at the edge of a woods.

"It's George!"

The titian-haired wig was gone and she appeared to be only semiconscious. Nancy and Bess leaped from the car and ran to her. As they shook George gently she opened her eyes.

"Nancy! Bess!" she murmured, and started weeping hysterically on Nancy's shoulder.

"Everything's all right, George," Nancy said.

Bess slipped a protective arm about the trembling girl's waist.

"Nancy, you must give up the case," George sobbed. "I insist!"

"Give it up?" Nancy echoed in disbelief. "Why, George, it's astounding to hear you suggest such a thing! You're the one who has been urging me to solve it."

The troopers had come up and were listening to the girls' conversation. Quickly Bess gave a glowing account of Nancy's brilliant sleuthing on the Velvet Gang case.

"That's amazing!" Lieutenant Whyte remarked. "If you track down the party thieves, my hat's off to you."

"But she mustn't do any more work on it," George mumbled.

Nancy and Bess exchanged glances. This was not the old George Fayne! What had happened?

CHAPTER VIII

Telltale Tag

APPARENTLY George had been badly frightened by her abductors, but after a good night's sleep she would be her normal self, Nancy figured.

Lieutenant Whyte knelt down beside George, and taking her wrist counted the girl's pulse beat. He puckered his brow.

"Tell me exactly what happened," he said.

"A woman leaned over me in the train and put a handkerchief over my nose and mouth. It smelled very sweet and made me black out."

"When did you first wake up?" Whyte asked.

"I don't know. What time is it?"

"I mean, did you wake up while you were in the car or after?" the officer questioned.

"There were voices— I—"

George stopped speaking and again lost consciousness. By the time they reached town George had revived somewhat and was examined by the police physician in his office. He said it was impossible to determine what drug had been administered to the girl but advised that she be taken home and put to bed for a few days.

"I'll phone Mother to come and get us," Bess offered.

When Nancy telephoned her father's hotel in Amstar to explain the delay, she was amazed to hear that he had checked out late that morning.

"Then the telegram *was* a hoax," she thought. "Those people certainly are clever. They were eavesdropping at my house and heard us making plans!"

She dialed her home and learned that Mr. Drew was in his law office. She called him there and explained what had happened.

"I don't like this at all," he said. "That gang is dangerous. You'd better forget the whole thing," he advised.

"But, Dad, you gave me a job to do and I want to finish it!" Nancy protested.

"Well, all right," he agreed reluctantly. "But do your sleuthing in safer places. You'll be home tonight?"

"Yes, Dad."

While waiting for Mrs. Marvin to arrive, Nancy decided to search at the railroad station for the object she had seen drop from the abductors' car.

"Oh, Nancy," George said weakly, "please don't do another thing about those awful people."

Seeing how deeply worried her friend was, Nancy decided she would not go. But a moment later George had dozed off on the couch in the physician's office.

"I'll be back before she wakes up," Nancy whispered to Bess and left the room.

Going directly to the railroad station, she spent twenty minutes searching along the tracks. Just as she was about to give up, her efforts were rewarded. Close to one of the steel rails lay a rectangular metal tag.

The young detective immediately recognized it as a charge plate issued by some department stores. The names and numbers on it had been flattened by a train passing over them, but the words "Tay" and "House Acc" were visible.

"Tay," Nancy mused. "I wonder if that could be Taylor's in River Heights. Maybe one of the thieves works there? Tomorrow I'll ask their credit manager if he can identify this house account charge plate."

Elated, Nancy returned to the doctor's office. George was still drowsing. Mrs. Marvin arrived in a little while and was very much concerned when she heard the details of what had happened. The physician assured her that the girl was well enough to travel but would probably sleep all the way home. He suggested George have no visitors for a couple days.

George awoke as the others were discussing the subject of masks. "Let's not talk about masks," she pleaded. "We've had enough of them forever!"

The subject was not mentioned again during the remainder of the trip to River Heights. George herself had little to say. Though she insisted that she felt fairly well, her face remained pale and she was shaky.

Nancy did not see her the next day. Mrs. Fayne kept her daughter in bed and allowed no visitors as the doctor had suggested. She reported that George had slept restlessly and had talked incoherently in her dreams, mostly about the Velvet Gang.

"Poor George!" Nancy thought unhappily. "It's really my fault! I never should have allowed her to masquerade as me."

On her way to see the credit manager of Taylor's Department Store, Nancy went over the thieves' activities. Since the night of the Becker wedding, no more robberies had been reported. Yet not for a moment did she believe that the thieves had left the vicinity. When the proper time arrived, they would strike again—possibly on the days indicated in the black hood.

Nancy was admitted to the office of Mr. Johnson, the credit manager of Taylor's. Without telling him of the previous day's experience, she mentioned a possible tie-in between the party thieves and the plate she carried.

Mr. Johnson examined the plate carefully. "It's one of ours all right," he said. "This was issued to an employee. But to tell you his or her name—that's impossible."

"Impossible?" Nancy asked, disappointed.

"Taylor's has several hundred employees to whom charge plates have been issued."

"You must have a record of every one," Nancy reminded him.

"We have. But the number of this plate has been obliterated. I couldn't interview all our workers on such slim evidence."

"I know how the checkup could be made without very much work," Nancy said.

"How?"

"By elimination. Ask all your employees to turn in their plates on a pretext of changing them. Naturally the person who lost this one wouldn't be able to."

Mr. Johnson considered the suggestion.

"You present your case very well, Miss Drew." He smiled. "I'll do it, even though it does inconvenience us."

Satisfied, Nancy next called at her father's office. He promptly put aside his work.

"Nothing new to report. Mr. Lightner came in to see me this morning. He's still worried about those threatened lawsuits. We're stalling for time. And what's your news?"

Nancy told him, then said she was going to follow Tombar that noon.

"At a safe distance," Mr. Drew cautioned. "And tell me, what do you hope to find out?"

Nancy explained about seeing Tombar bring a package from the entertainment company the same day the telltale cloak disappeared.

"He shook me off his trail rather pointedly when I followed him," she said. "And he's perfectly horrid about Linda without any reason. Maybe he's afraid she'll find out something."

"Better keep your suspicions to yourself until you have some evidence to back them up."

"I promise, Dad."

Nancy phoned Linda Seeley, who told her that Mr. Tombar had not come in that day.

"And the mysterious torn black cloak has never been returned," Linda reported. "But I have something else to tell you," she said. "Come over at lunchtime, will you?"

At noon the two girls met at a soda counter and sat down side by side. Linda said that everything was going well at the office.

"But I suppose something could happen at any time. Nancy, how would you like to attend a musicale?"

"When?"

"Tomorrow afternoon. At the Elkin home on

Kenwood Boulevard. The affair will be very plush. It's to introduce the French singer Madame De Velleaux."

"Is your company in charge?"

"Yes, and Mr. Lightner says he'll get you an invitation if you're interested. I'll be there."

Nancy decided instantly. She would enjoy the concert and there was the possibility that one of the party thieves might put in an appearance. Tomorrow would be the twenty-first of June, and 62| was one of the dates in the hood.

"Where shall I meet you, Linda?"

"I may have to go early," the other replied. "Tell you what! I'll send your invitation by messenger. Then if I'm held up, you won't be kept waiting at the door."

The next day, upon reaching the Elkin home, Nancy presented her invitation to the butler at the front entrance. The hall and living room were richly furnished and held many priceless art objects. She went upstairs and laid her light coat on one of the beds. As far as Nancy could observe, there was not a single plainclothesman on duty.

She went downstairs and lingered near the front door so that she could scrutinize all new arrivals. A few minutes later Nancy caught sight of Peter Tombar. He saw her at the same moment and came over.

"Well, well," he said with false geniality, "so you're an admirer of Madame De Velleaux?"

"I've never heard her sing," Nancy replied. "Is Linda Seeley here?"

"Linda isn't coming," he said shortly.

"Is she ill?"

"No. She was needed elsewhere. I sent her to another house. I'm taking over here myself."

Nancy remained silent, wondering whether the excuse he had given was really what lay behind Linda's failure to appear.

"How did you get in?" Tombar asked Nancy abruptly.

"By invitation."

"And where did you get the invitation?" the man growled. "Your name wasn't on the guest list."

Nancy smiled sweetly. "Perhaps you didn't look carefully enough."

Deciding not to give the man an opportunity to question her further, Nancy sauntered away. She entered the music room and seated herself in the last row near the door. A few minutes later the concert began.

After sitting there long enough to make it appear that she had come only to hear the singer, Nancy left to start her sleuthing. She tiptoed out and stood in the main hall a moment. The other rooms on the lower floor appeared to be deserted.

Meeting one of the maids, she asked her if she knew what had become of the man from the Lightner Entertainment Company.

"No, miss, I don't," the maid replied. "I've been upstairs. The only person up there is the sick lady."

"Someone ill?"

"Yes, miss. One of the guests. Just a few minutes ago she asked me to get her a cup of tea from the kitchen. I'm going for it now."

"Where is the lady?"

"In the bedroom where the guests left their coats."

The maid hastened to the kitchen. Nancy hesitated a moment, mulling over the information. Was the woman really ill? The errand might have been a way to get rid of the maid!

Silently Nancy mounted the stairway to the bedroom and opened the partly closed door. A slim woman stood at the dresser, hurriedly removing jewelry from the top drawer!

In the mirror Nancy caught a fleeting glimpse of a hard, brazen face. She knew instantly that she had seen the woman before. The Hendricks' ball perhaps? Yes, that was it! This was the woman who had worn the Javanese costume!

Now Nancy had caught her red-handed. She must bar the exit and call for help!

Before she could turn, Nancy was suddenly

grasped from behind. She tried to scream, but it was choked off as a large hand was clamped over her mouth.

Shoved roughly into the room, she was pushed face down, among the summer wraps on the bed and pinned in a viselike grip.

CHAPTER IX

Indelible Evidence

"Good work!" Nancy heard the woman thief exclaim. "Serves the little sneak right!"

"I thought something was amiss up here," replied her male accomplice, speaking with an exaggerated English accent.

Still maintaining a tight hold on Nancy, her captor chuckled softly. "I fancy she'll not interfere again soon."

His partner removed an armful of the coats and jackets, then rolled the bedspread tightly around Nancy. The woman piled the clothing on top of her.

"Make sure she won't meddle any more!" the woman cried.

"No time, my dear," the man answered. "We shall be forced to make a hasty exit. The maid will be returning."

"Then cut out that silly accent and let's get out of here!" his companion muttered.

Just when Nancy thought she surely would suffocate, the man suddenly released his grip. The couple raced from the room.

Nancy struggled to untangle herself from the heavy bedspread and its burden of coats. When she finally got to her feet and stepped into the hall, the man and woman were not in sight. Just then the maid who had gone for the tea opened a door from the back stairway.

"Gracious!" she exclaimed, staring at Nancy. "What happened to you?"

For the first time Nancy realized how disheveled she must look. Her dress was rumpled and her hair mussed.

"The woman who pretended to be ill is a thief! She and some man tried to smother me. Did you see anyone running out?"

"No, miss," the startled maid replied, setting her tray on a hall table.

Nancy said, "Maybe they're hiding in one of the bedrooms. Come on. Let's look for them!"

They searched the bedrooms, looking in closets and every possible hiding place until they were satisfied no one remained on the second floor. Nancy combed her hair and smoothed her dress before going downstairs. In the kitchen she found Tombar directing the caterers.

"Guests aren't allowed in here," he said icily.

Nancy was not intimidated. "I came to get a sandwich," she said, picking up one from a tray. "I'm simply starved."

She smiled and closed the door. At that moment a burst of applause indicated that the musicale was ending. A moment later the guests began going toward the dining room for tea.

Nancy located the hostess, introduced herself, and whispered what had happened.

"I don't know whether that woman took anything or not," she said. "You'd better check."

Together they went upstairs. Mrs. Elkin said that she disliked parties with detectives standing around and had refused to have any.

"Every person on my list is a friend," she said. "I don't see how a thief could have slipped in."

Mrs. Elkin cried out in dismay when she discovered that several pieces of valuable jewelry were missing. She immediately called the police, who offered to send a woman plainclothes detective.

"I may have a clue," Nancy said as they were waiting. "Possibly the thief left a coat here that will identify her."

When the woman detective arrived from headquarters, she took charge of the coats. The hostess was asked to identify each guest as she came for her wrap. Finally all the coats had been claimed except a long blue linen one with large pockets.

Nancy struggled to untangle herself

"The owner is not coming for this coat, that's evident!" Nancy said. "My guess is it was worn by the thief!"

Picking it up, she examined the coat for clues. In one pocket was a make-up kit. The other contained a velvet hooded mask! Nancy tore open the stitching of the lining. There were no numbers on this mask.

The policewoman ripped the lining of the coat. Nothing had been hidden inside, and the garment had no marks of identification.

"I'll take the coat, mask, and kit to headquarters," she said.

After Nancy reached home, Linda Seeley telephoned to apologize for her absence from the musicale.

"Mr. Tombar sent me on a trifling errand instead," she explained. "I guess he thought I wasn't capable of handling the affair."

Nancy remarked that Mr. Tombar himself had not performed too efficiently and told of the robbery.

"Oh, how dreadful!" Linda cried.

After the phone call, Nancy sat lost in thought. Suddenly an idea came to her. She would have a chemical analysis made of the ink notations which she had discovered on the lining of the first hooded mask.

In the morning she went to a laboratory and was informed by one of the chemists that the fluid was rather uncommon. It was new and was sold exclusively for marking garments.

"Then any number of dry cleaners might have similar ink?" Nancy asked.

"Not necessarily," the chemist replied. "This particular type of ink is pretty expensive."

Nancy was excited. Did the Lightner Entertainment Company use it? she wondered. At noon she found Linda at the drugstore soda counter and asked her how costumes and masks were marked.

"Oh, we use a special indelible ink that lasts forever," Linda replied.

"Could you let me borrow a bottle of it?"

"Why, I guess so. How soon do you want it, Nancy?"

"Right away if possible."

"Wait here and I'll see if I can slip one out of the supply room," Linda said.

Ten minutes later she returned with the bottle of ink tucked in an office envelope. As she gave it to Nancy, Peter Tombar entered the drugstore.

He could not possibly have known what the fat envelope contained, because Nancy thrust it quickly into her handbag. Nevertheless, he regarded the two girls intently, then walked over to the soda counter.

"Miss Seeley, you are five minutes over your lunch hour," he said.

"I'm sorry, Mr. Tombar. I—I was just leaving."

"Leaving? I thought you were just coming. Didn't you hand—?"

"Are you eating here?" Nancy broke in.

Tombar glared at her but did not reply. Linda took advantage of the moment to escape.

Nancy regretted the meeting with Tombar. He could not possibly know what Linda had given her, but he might be suspicious.

No sooner had Tombar left the drugstore than Nancy returned to the laboratory. She gave the chemist the bottle of ink for analysis and waited for his report.

Finally it came. She was informed that the fluid was identical to the one used to write the numbers on the lining of the hooded mask.

"What a clue!" Nancy thought, and hurried from the laboratory to return the bottle to Linda.

Nancy talked with Linda for a few minutes. Then, just as she managed to slip her the envelope with the bottle in it, Tombar entered from a back room. He stopped short when he saw the two girls.

"Miss Seeley," he said coldly, "I suggest that you return to the work you left. I will help Miss Drew."

"Never mind," Nancy said quickly. "I'm just going!" She sailed out cheerfully, but her heart was thumping uncomfortably. Had the man seen the bottle change hands?

On Sunday she told her father about the ink clue. "Now I'm positive someone at Lightner's is a member of the gang," Nancy said. "If I could only work there a few days, I could watch everyone."

"Couldn't you help Linda with the office work? I'm sure Mr. Lightner would give his permission."

Nancy's father called the man's home. After a brief conversation he said good-by. "It's all settled," Mr. Drew reported. "Mr. Lightner was most agreeable to the suggestion."

Nancy appeared punctually at the Lightner Entertainment Company at nine o'clock Monday morning. She noted, with some amusement, Tombar's reaction to her arrival. After his first unfriendly stare, he pointedly ignored Nancy.

Nancy spent an uneventful morning sorting letters and rearranging files. Whenever she was about to seize an opportunity to slip into the storerooms to look for clues, Tombar would suddenly appear again.

"He may not be speaking to me, but he's surely keeping an eye on my whereabouts," Nancy thought. "I'll hold off until lunchtime. While he's out, I can do some looking around."

But when twelve o'clock came, the assistant manager did not leave, nor did he at one. To Nancy's dismay, she observed him eating sandwiches right at his desk.

"Evidently he doesn't intend to budge from here today," Nancy said to herself.

This proved to be true. By late afternoon Nancy was weary from hunger. Her eyes ached from the tedious filing, and she was discouraged.

When five o'clock came, Nancy left the Lightner offices without seeing Linda. Right after supper, however, Nancy received an urgent telephone call from the girl.

"It's happened!" she announced dramatically. "And I don't know what to do!"

"Another robbery?" Nancy gasped.

"No, not that. I've been discharged!"

CHAPTER X

A New Ruse

LINDA poured out the story of her dismissal by Mr. Tombar, who had given her no chance to defend herself.

"He made an inventory check late Saturday. Just a single little bottle of ink that was opened without his permission! But did he ever make a fuss! He suspected me right away."

"You didn't tell him you lent me the ink?"

"No, but from the way he questioned me, I think he guessed it. Anyway, he made me admit that I had taken the bottle from the shelf. I offered to pay for a full one, but he wouldn't even listen. He just told me I was through."

"Now, Linda, don't feel too bad," Nancy comforted her. "Take it easy for a few days and I'll help you get your job back or find another—a better one where there will be no Mr. Tombar."

"Oh, Nancy, you're so kind!" Linda exclaimed and thanked her.

Though Nancy sounded confident, she was troubled. Now that Linda had been discharged there would be no source of information at the entertainment company. To make matters worse, Mr. Lightner himself called in a few minutes to say that affairs at the office were a bit confused at the moment and perhaps Nancy had better not return to work there since Linda was gone.

"I'm sorry," Nancy said. "But it will be all right if I drop in, won't it? I'd like to talk to you about several things."

"Any time."

After she had hung up, Nancy sat lost in thought. No mystery she had ever tried to solve had baffled her more. In addition, George Fayne had not recovered from her frightening experience.

"I feel simply terrible about it," Nancy told Hannah Gruen. "George is weak and has no appetite. But what's even worse, she mopes around talking about the party thieves and every time I see her she begs me to give up the case."

"Those criminals probably threatened her," Hannah suggested.

Nancy nodded. "It would explain her pleas to me to drop the case," Nancy conceded.

The following morning she decided to see Mr.

Lightner about Linda. As Nancy drove downtown her thoughts went to George again.

"Something must be done about her!" Nancy decided as she parked in front of the entertainment company building. "If I solve the mystery, that may do it."

She went at once to Mr. Lightner's office. He listened politely to her request that he take Linda back but shook his head.

"Usually I leave employment matters in that department entirely to Mr. Tombar," he said. "If he discharged Linda, there must have been a good reason."

"It was really my fault, Mr. Lightner," said Nancy, and explained about asking Linda to borrow the ink bottle. "If she hadn't been trying to help me, it never would have happened."

"That does change the picture somewhat," the company president admitted. "But perhaps Mr. Tombar had other reasons as well. After all, the girl has been under suspicion."

"Unjustly so, I'm sure, Mr. Lightner. She wasn't even at that musicale where there was a robbery."

"I know," Mr. Lightner said. "But there were other parties and certain thefts right here which raised doubts as to her honesty."

"If I could prove she's innocent, would you take Linda back?" Nancy asked.

"Why—uh—yes. Of course, that is, with Mr. Tombar's okay."

Nancy realized that Linda would need a reference to secure a new job. She could not get one from her ex-employer.

Nancy thought quickly. She could only help Linda by catching the thieves! Nancy must get an invitation to the affair on June twenty-sixth.

"Mr. Lightner," she said, "you know, of course, that I've been trying to help Dad solve the mystery of the party thieves."

The man smiled. "Yes, he told me even I was under suspicion for a time!"

"May I go to the lecture at the Claytons'?" Nancy asked.

He readily gave his consent, telling her to meet him there at seven-thirty Wednesday evening.

"I'm taking personal charge," he informed her. "I've decided it's high time I did a little investigating of my own."

"Then Mr. Tombar won't be there?"

"No," Mr. Lightner replied. "He's in a huff about it, too. But that's beside the point."

Further conversation revealed that Peter Tombar was annoyed also because Mr. Lightner had asked him not to take such long lunch hours.

Nancy smiled. "The man must have been driving out into the country a good deal," she thought. "Well, if he doesn't do that any more, another clue is washed out."

Speaking again of the lecture, she suggested that as a precautionary measure all the cards of admission be marked with a special swirl. Then no uninvited person could possibly slip in without being detected. Mr. Lightner immediately agreed to Nancy's proposal.

"I have the list here, ready for addressing," he told her. "Shall we mark them now? I'll have a messenger deliver them this evening."

The work was done quickly. Each card was marked on the reverse side.

"It's essential that we tell no one what we've done," Nancy advised Mr. Lightner. "Not even your secretary or Mr. Tombar."

"Surely both of them can be trusted."

"Nevertheless, let's keep this as our own secret."

"Very well," Mr. Lightner said. "I'll personally check every invitation at the door."

After lunch Nancy went to Mr. Johnson's office to inquire what progress had been made in recalling the charge plates. She learned that they were coming in very slowly. He said that he did not dare push the matter, lest any dishonest employee get an inkling of what lay behind the scheme.

"I'll let you know if anything turns up," the credit manager promised.

Nancy had a long talk with her father. Mr. Drew said he had decided to take the Lightner case, thanks to his daughter's fine sleuthing. But the company owner refused to believe that any of his present employees were dishonest.

"His clients are getting a bit impatient and want to start their suits," Mr. Drew revealed, "but we're stalling for time."

"If I could only discover something worth while!" Nancy sighed.

She spent the rest of the day with George, who had sent for her. The listless girl was in no better spirits and Nancy missed her friend's help in sleuthing. All she could do was humor George.

Bess was out of town, leaving Nancy with a lonesome feeling.

"But I mustn't give up, even for a second," she determined.

The distraught George again begged Nancy to give up the case. "You—you simply must stop working on it," she pleaded.

"George, whatever has happened to you?" Nancy asked. "This case is no different from others I've worked on."

"It's much more dangerous. Nancy, please—"

The young sleuth patted George's hand. "I'll be careful, really I will," she promised. "Tomorrow I'm going to a perfectly safe highbrow lecture!"

The next evening Nancy arrived at the Clayton home early. To her chagrin she found Tombar there.

"It wasn't necessary for him to be here," Mr.

Lightner told Nancy. "But he insisted I might run into difficulty handling some of the details I wasn't used to."

Nancy smiled and made no comment. It was obvious to her that Tombar wanted to be there! Making a great show of directing the placement of chairs, he bustled about, growling orders at everyone.

Mr. Lightner had posted himself at the front door to inspect each card that was presented. Nancy stood close by to scrutinize the arriving guests. Everyone seemed straightforward-looking and above suspicion.

"So far so good," Mr. Lightner presently whispered to Nancy. "At least two-thirds of the cards are in. All are authentic."

Nancy had observed a man loitering outdoors near the parking lot. She called Mr. Lightner's attention to him.

"Oh, don't worry about him. He's a private detective I employed. After the program starts, he'll move inside and help keep an eye on everyone."

In a few minutes the lecture began. Not all the cards had been turned in, so Mr. Lightner remained at the front door to meet latecomers.

"It looks as if the party thieves aren't going to show up," Nancy remarked. "Just to be sure no one is prowling about the garden, I'll walk around outside."

She circled the house, noting that all the windows on the first floor wcre very high above the ground. It would be difficult to climb in and dangerous to drop from any of them!

In her tour Nancy presently came to the parking area and wandered among the cars. Approaching a long black sedan, she was startled to see a man lying on the ground, almost under the front wheels.

"Oh," she thought, "he's ill!"

Kneeling, she realized that he was unconscious. As wild ideas raced through Nancy's mind, she received a further shock. All the lights in the Clayton house suddenly went out!

CHAPTER XI

Loot for Sale

NANCY felt it would be cruel to leave the man who lay unconscious on the ground. Yet she wanted to return to the suddenly darkened house. She was sure another robbery was in progress!

As Nancy leaned over the stranger, she noticed a peculiar sweet-smelling odor on his clothing. Instantly she thought of George's experience on the train.

"This man has been drugged just as she was!" Nancy decided. "And by the same people! They must be in the house!"

Repeatedly she called for help but no one came. Probably the people in the house could not hear her. Minutes later the lights went on again.

"If only someone would come here so I could leave!" Nancy thought unhappily. "The thieves are probably making a getaway this very minute."

She hoped that members of the Velvet Gang would try to escape through the parking area, giving her a chance to intercept them. But time passed and no one came that way.

Nancy chafed the stranger's wrists and presently he groaned. "Help!" he cried out feebly. Then he noticed Nancy and stared blankly into her face. "Where am I?" he mumbled.

"You're in the parking area at the Claytons'," Nancy told him. "Can you sit up?"

"I think so," he said weakly. Carefully she helped him to a sitting position.

"That's better," he muttered. "I'll be all right."

"Can you recall what happened to you?" Nancy asked.

"It's coming back now," he said, brushing a hand across his eyes. "As I got out of the car I was grabbed from behind. A handkerchief with a peculiar odor was pressed to my face."

"Your wallet. Do you still have it?"

The guest fumbled in his pocket. "Gone," he admitted ruefully. "I've been robbed."

"Did it contain anything besides money?" Nancy asked.

"Yes—several cards, including the lecture invitation."

The stranger identified himself as Albert G. Brunner and said he had come alone. Nancy introduced herself and told him of her suspicions.

She offered to help Mr. Brunner into the house, saying a doctor should be summoned.

Nancy managed to assist the man the short distance to the house. There she was relieved of his care by two solicitous servants.

Instantly Nancy sought Mr. Lightner. But even he believed the darkness had been a temporary power shutoff.

An investigation was started at once. It revealed that valuable silver pieces and figurines were missing from the first floor and jewelry from the second.

"This will ruin me!" Mr. Lightner confided to Nancy.

"Surely it isn't that bad," Nancy said soothingly. "By the way, where is Mr. Tombar?"

"I haven't seen him. I suppose he's out looking for those thieves."

Nancy decided to find out for herself. Checking room after room, she finally located him in the kitchen, giving instructions to the caterers. Nancy watched Tombar until he was free, then casually started talking to him about the theft.

"I was outdoors and didn't see a thing," she said chattily. "How about you?"

"Say, what is this, a third degree?" Tombar snapped at her, and stalked off.

There was nothing more she could do. The police had arrived and taken charge. Nancy listened as they made the usual checkup. The same robbery pattern as before! Not a clue left by the wily party thieves!

On the way home Nancy thought about the Velvet Gang. They would never be caught by ordinary methods. They were too clever at anticipating the traps laid for them.

Nancy's thoughts also turned to Tombar. The man was an enigma. He was certainly faithful to his job, and since he knew nothing about the marked invitations, he could not have tipped off the thieves about them.

"Still I don't trust him," Nancy said to herself. "I wish I could go to that wedding Friday night. Then I could watch Tombar myself. But I can't refuse to attend Helen Tyne's dance at this late date. And Ned would never forgive me if I disappointed him."

Next morning at breakfast Nancy was turning over several plans of action in her mind when Bess Marvin arrived.

"Hi, Nancy!" she said but did not smile.

"Hello, yourself, welcome back. What's wrong, Bess? You don't usually get over here so early."

"It's George. The doctor says she's still suffering the effects of that frightening kidnapping episode. Personally, I think it's more than that. George is scared out of her wits about something."

"She never was frightened of anything before."

"I know," Bess admitted soberly. "Something

strange has come over her—it's as if she were under a spell. Won't you talk to her? For some reason, she's especially troubled about you."

"Me?" Nancy echoed, surprised. A few minutes later they left the house to call on George.

The girl did not look ill, although she was propped against pillows in a living-room chair. After Nancy had chatted with her a few minutes, however, she knew that Bess was right.

"What happened last night?" George asked anxiously. "I read about the robbery in the paper. I'm sure you were there."

"Yes."

"Nancy, I asked you to give up the case! You don't understand what you're up against. Those fiends will stop at nothing—nothing—" George cried out hysterically.

Bess and Nancy soothed their friend as best they could, but Nancy would not promise to give up her sleuthing completely. Mrs. Fayne came in to attend her daughter, and a few minutes afterward the girls left.

"Just seeing me seems to excite poor George," Nancy remarked when she and Bess reached the sidewalk.

"We must avoid talking about the mystery when we're with her," Bess suggested.

"But she's the one who always brings it up," Nancy said with a sigh. "Bess, this is awful."

"I know. Maybe you ought to give up the case

—or at least pretend to. Then maybe George will get better."

"I'll follow your advice," Nancy promised. "I'll do a good pretending job. Right now, I'm going to Taylor's. Want to come along?"

"Sure."

They called on Mr. Johnson to ask about the return of employees' charge plates.

"Not many more have come in," he reported. "We're too busy to go around collecting them. Sorry. I'll let you know what happens."

Nancy was deeply disappointed by his lack of interest. "I can't understand it," she told Bess. "He doesn't seem to care whether he has a thief working for him or not."

As they passed the jewelry counter, Nancy caught sight of Alice Tompson, a former classmate, who had recently taken a job at Taylor's. The three girls chatted for a few minutes. Nancy asked Alice if she had turned in her charge plate as requested by the management.

"Why, no," Alice replied. "I was going to, but then a note came around changing the order."

"Changing it! Why?"

"I don't know. It just said we weren't to send the plates in after all."

"So that's why so few were returned," Nancy mused. "I wonder if Mr. Johnson himself sent out the order."

Curious to know the truth, she and Bess immediately returned to the credit manager's office. Mr. Johnson was elsewhere in the store, but his secretary assured the girls that the order had not come from him.

"If I were you, though, I wouldn't bother him about it," she advised. "He has an important conference today. The entire matter is annoying to him."

Nancy felt completely frustrated. It was such a good chance to catch the thief and it was being thrown away!

"I guess I'll have to give up the idea," she admitted to Bess.

"Oh, you'll think up some other scheme," her friend said loyally.

With time on their hands, the girls walked idly through the store. Bess looked at blouses and selected one. Finally they returned to the jewelry department to purchase a birthday gift for Mrs. Marvin.

"A new assortment of art objects just came in this morning. I've been arranging them in a showcase," Alice told Bess. "We have a lovely miniature painted on porcelain. I'll show it to you."

"I'm afraid that would be too expensive—"

"Not this one." Alice smiled. "The price, in my opinion, is ridiculously low. In fact, I was amazed when I saw the tag. Come and look at it."

She led the girls to a counter on which a number of small gifts were displayed. One of them was a miniature of Marie Antoinette.

Nancy drew in her breath, stunned. She could not believe the sight before her eyes. The lovely picture looked exactly like the one which had been stolen from Gloria Hendrick's home!

CHAPTER XII

Clever Detection

"THIS must be the stolen miniature!" Nancy gasped.

"It might be a copy," Bess suggested.

"It doesn't look like a copy," Nancy insisted. "The gold frame has a number of tiny scratches on it as if it were old. Bess, I'm sure this was stolen from the Hendricks' collection."

The two girls examined the miniature in detail, and Nancy told of having seen it before the robbery.

"But, Nancy, Taylor's wouldn't accept stolen merchandise," Alice objected.

"Not knowingly. But this may have been sold to them without their realizing it was stolen. Perhaps they got it from an antique dealer."

All agreed that the miniature was greatly underpriced, even if it were only an excellent copy of the original. Nancy promptly bought the miniature. She would find out for certain if it had been stolen from the Hendricks.

"Have you others like these?" Nancy asked.

"I know a shipment came in, but all the merchandise isn't on the floor yet," Alice replied. "I'll ask Mr. Watkins about it. He's head of our department."

Mr. Watkins was a stubby, white-haired man with glasses. When he saw the miniature which was being wrapped for Nancy, he glanced quickly at the tag.

"This item must have been mismarked," he said. "Taylor's wouldn't ask you to pay more, of course, but I must check invoices before any other articles in the shipment are sold."

Nancy expressed a desire to see the other miniatures.

"We'll look into this," the elderly man said. "Come with me to the marking room."

He led Nancy and Bess to a rear exit and across an alleyway to a building used for receiving.

"Snecker!" he called loudly, switching on an overhead light. "Hey, Snecker!" As a young clerk emerged from an adjoining room, Mr. Watkins asked, "Where is he?"

"He's not here," the boy said. "Mr. Snecker's taken the day off."

"Again?" Mr. Watkins remarked irritably.

He explained to Nancy and Bess that Ralph

Snecker was in charge of uncrating and marking all items to be put on sale, and shipping damaged goods back to factories.

"Then if a mistake were made in pricing the miniature, it would be Mr. Snecker's fault?" Nancy asked.

"That's right. This miniature is underpriced —no question about that. I'll examine the invoices."

Nancy and Bess waited patiently in a windowless stuffy room while he checked through records and bills. Crates and boxes were piled all about, many not yet opened.

"Strange," Mr. Watkins remarked presently. "I can't seem to find an invoice for the piece you have. I know a small shipment came in from abroad." He questioned the clerk, but the young man knew nothing about the miniature.

"I'll take it up with Mr. Snecker tomorrow," Mr. Watkins said.

"Is he an old and trusted employee?" Nancy asked casually.

"No, he hasn't been with Taylor's very long," Mr. Watkins admitted. "However, he's an efficient worker. Takes too many days off, though. Either he's ill or he has to go fishing. The minute he's through work, away he goes to the country."

Mr. Watkins was still checking through a stack of papers in search of the invoice.

"The fishing bug bit Snecker hard. Why, he goes out to the river summer and winter, clear, rainy, or snowy!"

This struck Nancy as odd. How did the man manage to keep up with his work? She thought she had better meet and question him soon, since it seemed probable he might be dismissed before long. She decided to return to the store the next day.

Meanwhile, she and Bess called at the Hendricks' home. When Gloria and her mother saw the miniature they instantly identified it as theirs.

"The idea of Taylor's selling stolen merchandise!" Mrs. Hendrick exclaimed indignantly. "Wait until I tell the police!"

"I have a hunch the store isn't to blame," said Nancy.

"Well, anyhow, you got one of our treasures back," Gloria spoke up. "You're so clever, Nancy!"

The young detective shook her head modestly. "There's a lot of work to do on this case yet."

Mrs. Hendrick smiled. "Don't worry, dear. I'm sure you'll solve it."

Next morning Nancy hurried to the department store. To her disappointment, Snecker had telephoned that he was too ill to work.

"Very likely he's out fishing," Mr. Watkins grumbled.

During the brief conversation with the elderly man, Nancy learned that the note sent to employees countermanding the order to turn in their charge plates had been unsigned. At once she became suspicious and her thoughts turned to Snecker and the stolen miniature.

"Do you know where Mr. Snecker lives?" Nancy asked Mr. Watkins.

He consulted a book under the counter. "Twenty-four Tanner Street."

Nancy thanked Mr. Watkins for the information and left the store. She stopped to ask a traffic policeman the way to Tanner Street. He gave directions to a section of town with which she was not familiar.

After riding through several drab, unattractive streets, Nancy finally came to the one she sought. The Snecker house was at the far end of it. The red-brick dwelling was run-down and old.

Nancy applied the brakes, intending to pull into a vacant space a short distance beyond the building. As she slowed down, another car which had been parked directly in front of the four-story house pulled away from the curb.

"Now, where have I seen that car before?" Nancy thought.

Her pulse quickened. The car was a mud-splattered green sedan. Though she caught only a fleeting glimpse of the driver, she recognized him at once.

"That's Peter Tombar!" she thought. "Has he been at Ralph Snecker's? And why?"

Nancy wanted to follow Tombar. She might pick up a clue!

But almost at once she discarded the idea in favor of calling on Snecker. She had an excuse which she could not use another time—one which might prove helpful in solving the mystery.

Nancy parked at the curb and went into the apartment-house vestibule. She pressed a buzzer above the name of Ralph Snecker. In a moment a shrill feminine voice answered through the tube.

"Who's there?"

"I'm from Taylor's," Nancy replied, purposely not giving her name.

The woman seemed a trifle flustered. "I'll be right down."

In a moment a tall woman appeared, breathing heavily from her haste. She had a determined chin and narrow blue eyes.

"Are you Mrs. Snecker?" Nancy asked politely.

"I am," she replied, eyeing the girl warily. "The store sent you, you said?"

"I came to inquire about your husband. We're worried concerning his absence."

"I know, I know," the woman said impatiently. "They always send some busybody around to ask questions. Well, you can tell 'em he's sick again!"

"I'm sorry to hear that. Nothing serious, I hope."

"He's in bed with the asthma. I tell 'im if he'd stay away from the river he wouldn't get these attacks. He's supposed to take some medicine, but how can he when we don't have no money?"

Nancy feigned concern. "You're having a hard time of it, aren't you?"

"Whadda ya expect on his salary? Maybe he ain't no hustler, if you know what I mean. I tell 'im he ought to ask for more, but—"

Mrs. Snecker's tirade was interrupted by a loud call from up the stairway.

"Florence! Florence! Come here, will you?"

"That's 'im callin' me now," Mrs. Snecker said. "He's a nuisance when he's sick. Always keepin' me on the run. He wants me to wait on 'im like a baby."

Nancy could see that the woman was completely out of sorts.

"You needn't tell the store what I just said," Mrs. Snecker advised hastily. "I shouldn't 'a' spoke my piece, but Ralph's got me down with his gripes and complaints. When he works, things ain't so bad. Oh, well, we'll soon be out of these shabby quarters."

"You're moving to a better apartment?"

"You bet we are."

"But I thought you just said Mr. Snecker's salary isn't large and he's not a go-getter."

"Not at store business, he ain't. But he's got another line he's workin'." Mrs. Snecker dropped her voice, so that it could not possibly carry upstairs. "We'll soon be on easy street, struttin' with the best of 'em!"

"Like your friend Tombar?"

"Sure, and believe me—"

Mrs. Snecker suddenly broke off, staring suspiciously at Nancy. Belatedly it dawned on her that she had talked too freely. Without another word she slammed the door in Nancy's face!

CHAPTER XIII

Blue Iris Inn

ANGRY, Nancy knocked on the door, because she wanted to talk to Mr. Snecker very much. But his wife refused to open it.

"Go away!" she screamed.

"Oh, well," Nancy thought, returning to her car, "I learned something. The Sneckers and Tombar are friends!"

As she drove through the downtown section of River Heights, Nancy also reflected on the remark that the woman had made about Snecker's other work that would put them "on easy street." Did it include Tombar?

That evening when Ned called for Nancy she floated downstairs in a sheer yellow formal with gold accessories.

"What a doll!" exclaimed her handsome escort. "All ready for fun!"

"Maybe trouble, too," said Nancy and reminded him that it was the twenty-eighth, one of the dates in the hood. But her worry was needless. No robbery took place.

On Monday morning she went to see Mr. Lightner. He was in excellent spirits.

"The wedding on Friday, Miss Drew, went off like clockwork. No thefts or even attempted ones."

"I know," said Nancy. "The newspapers did not mention burglaries at any other parties either. But it doesn't prove that the thieves have ceased their activities," she reminded him. "They know the police are on their trail, so they may have decided to lie low for a while. Today may tell the tale. It's the first of July—"

"Yes, I understand," the company president cut in. "Linda told me about the dates in the mask. Tonight there's a big dance at the John Dwight estate."

"I think it would be a good idea if I attended that party," said Nancy.

Mr. Lightner agreed and promised to arrange the invitation.

"Linda knew a great deal about your work, didn't she?" Nancy asked. As the man nodded, she remarked, "I should think you'd miss her."

"Well, yes, we do."

"Then why not take her back?"

Mr. Lightner frowned. "You'll have to discuss

that with Mr. Tombar," he said. "I can't interfere. He handles all such matters."

"But have I your permission to talk to him
about her?"

"Certainly. Go ahead. I don't think you'll get
very far, though."

Nancy shared this opinion. Nevertheless, she
felt that it would not do any harm to talk with
Tombar about Linda. She went to the wardrobe
rooms.

"He's busy and I have no idea how long he'll
be tied up," his secretary informed her.

"That's all right. I'll wait."

Tombar was talking loudly. Nancy, seated in
a chair near the door, could not help overhearing
his angry voice.

"No, I won't do it!" Tombar exclaimed. "Quit
trying to persuade me. I wish you wouldn't keep
pestering me. I've told you before never to
bother me when I'm on the job. This time I
mean it."

His visitor's reply was so soft-spoken that
Nancy could not catch what he was saying.

But she heard every word of Tombar's angry
outburst. "Get out of here, Harris!" he roared.
"Get out of here before I throw you out!"

The door was flung open and Mr. Harris
rushed out so fast that Nancy did not get a view
of his face. She was confronted by Tombar's beet-
red face. He sprang toward her, shaking his fist.

"You here again!" he exclaimed. "You little eavesdropper! Spying on me! Well, I won't have it!"

Though furious at Tombar's outburst, Nancy gave no indication of her feeling.

"Spying?" she echoed. "I'm sure I don't know what you mean."

"You're always around!" Tombar snapped.

Nancy smiled and remained silent.

"Well, since you're so curious," the man said, "I'll tell you why Richard Harris was here. He's trying to sell me a cemetery plot, and I don't want to buy it. That's all."

Nancy was certain that the man was lying, but she pretended to accept his explanation. Quickly she explained the purpose of her call—to ask that he take Linda Seeley back. She gave several reasons why the girl should be rehired, but the man, who by now had calmed down somewhat, gazed at her coldly.

"I have someone else in mind," he stated.

The telephone rang, and Tombar stepped to his desk to answer it. Though he lowered his voice, Nancy heard the name Florence. Instantly her suspicions were aroused. Was he talking to Florence Snecker?

Try as she would, Nancy could not figure out anything about the call because the conversation was one-sided, the other person doing all the talking. Finally he slammed down the receiver, and turning almost purple with rage, glared at Nancy in the doorway.

"I knew it! Trying to get an earful again!" he shouted. "Well, this is the last time!"

He started toward Nancy as if intending to harm her. Midway across the room he stopped in dismay, staring over her shoulder.

Nancy turned. Directly behind her stood Mr. Lightner, glowering at his employee.

"What's going on here?" he demanded.

"Why, I—that is—Miss Drew is always interfering—" Tombar stammered.

"That's no excuse for your actions, Tombar."

"I—I'm sorry, Mr. Lightner. My apologies. I didn't mean any harm. I—I—"

Nancy escaped to the hall so that the two men might talk privately. But they did not close the door, and she could hear them plainly.

"Tombar, I've given you free rein in the business," Mr. Lightner said icily. "I permitted you to take complete charge in this department. Without my knowledge you discharged Miss Seeley, though personally I liked her work.

"And since then matters in this department have been no better—if anything, they're worse. Records in bad shape. Customers dissatisfied.

"And now I hear you threatening Miss Drew, who happens to be the daughter of one of my very good friends. This is the last straw."

"I gave an apology."

"It is accepted," Mr. Lightner retorted, "and also your resignation."

"My resignation! You can't do that. I've been here four years and people depend on me—!"

"I can and I have," Mr. Lightner corrected. "Pick up your paycheck as you leave. There is nothing more to discuss."

Mr. Lightner turned on his heel and left the office. Meeting Nancy in the hall he assured her that she was welcome to return at any time, and he was sorry for what had happened.

"I know it wasn't your fault," Mr. Lightner said.

He promised that he would look into Linda's case as soon as he had the time. Nancy thanked him and started for the door.

At that moment she saw Tombar stride out of the building by a side entrance. He had not waited for his paycheck!

"That will give him an excuse to come back here later," she thought, and left the building.

Her next stop was her father's office. Through him she learned that Mr. Harris, instead of being a cemetery-plot salesman, was connected with a downtown real-estate firm.

"I'm afraid Tombar is doing a lot of covering up," the lawyer stated. "Maybe I should have him followed."

"If he found out about it, we might never be able to prove what we suspect," Nancy said. "Give me a little longer, Dad. At least until you've finished the brief you're working on."

"Well, all right," her father agreed.

Obtaining Mr. Harris's address, Nancy went to his office. She told him quite frankly that she was a private detective and the purpose of her call was to learn of his business connection with Mr. Tombar. Still irritated by the treatment he had received, the agent willingly answered her query.

"I asked Tombar to sell the Blue Iris Inn," he disclosed. "Do you know the place?"

Nancy shook her head.

"It's a picturesque old inn out in the country on Woodland Road. An isolated place and in run-down condition. However, it could be converted into a topnotch dine-and-dance spot.

"I have a client who wants to develop the property. Tombar bought the place cheap and could make a neat profit on it."

"He doesn't want to sell it?" Nancy asked.

"We offered him double what he paid for it. He won't even discuss the matter."

"Maybe he plans to develop the place himself."

"Tombar?" Mr. Harris smiled. "I doubt it. He's just stubborn, that's all."

Nancy was sure that there was more than stubbornness back of the refusal. She asked the real-estate agent for a description of the old inn. He told her it was a clapboard structure, situated about eighteen miles from River Heights.

"I'll bet," Nancy reflected, "that's where Tombar used to go on his lunch hour."

Recalling the muddy tires on the man's car, she asked Mr. Harris if Woodland Road were paved.

"Not all the way. That's one of the bad features," the agent admitted. "My client· can finance the paving, though, for the short distance that would be necessary. Since it is fast falling into ruin, Tombar would be fortunate indeed to get rid of it now."

Nancy thanked the man for his information and said good-by.

The name Blue Iris Inn intrigued her. She would have enjoyed looking it over under any circumstances. Now, knowing its owner was Peter Tombar, she had a particular desire to see it.

As soon as she reached home she telephoned Bess Marvin. Nancy brought her up to date on what had happened and invited her to drive out to the Blue Iris Inn.

"Just the two of us? Alone?" Bess asked dubiously.

"Why, yes. Unless George can go. There's no chance of that, I suppose?"

"Don't even let her know you're making the trip," Bess advised hastily.

"I won't," Nancy promised, deeply concerned. "You'll go with me, though?"

"I suppose so," Bess consented reluctantly. "I

hate to do it, because I have a hunch we'll run into danger, but I won't let you down. When shall we start?"

"Right away. I'll stop for you in a few minutes." Nancy laughed, and added with a chuckle, "Better pack some sandwiches and a Thermos bottle of milk, too! The dining room won't be open at the Blue Iris Inn. And I predict we'll spend a long afternoon there!"

CHAPTER XIV

Nancy's Disguise

THE sun blazed overhead when Nancy and Bess finally came within view of the rambling old Blue Iris Inn.

The wooden building stood lonely and forlorn in a spot shaded by tall pines. Flower beds, including the iris from which the inn had taken its name, were choked with weeds.

After parking some distance from the inn, Nancy and Bess advanced cautiously in case Mr. Tombar should be around. Their attention was focused on the windows, all of which were boarded.

"This place gives me the creeps," Bess said. "It sure is no place to have a picnic."

Nancy laughed. "It really could be fixed up very attractively."

The girls circled the inn, peering through chinks in the boards which covered the windows.

To their amazement, they could see that most of the rooms on the lower floor were cluttered with boxes and crates, many of them with lids nailed shut.

"Looks like a warehouse," Bess remarked.

"I wonder if these came from Taylor's," Nancy said. "Snecker works in the receiving-and-marking room. And he's a friend of Tombar."

"Do you think they may contain stolen goods?"

"Maybe, Bess. I wish we could get inside and open one of those cases."

Nancy made a careful inspection of the windows, and tested every door. She quickly reached the conclusion that the building had been effectively barricaded.

"Let's leave, Nancy," Bess urged.

"I guess we'll have to." Nancy sighed. "But you know, Bess, this puzzle is beginning to take a definite form.

"Remember the charge plate that I found on the railroad track? Well, it must have belonged to Snecker. Now, unless those cartons contain Blue Iris furnishings, I'm convinced there's something fishy about their being here."

"I think so too, Nancy. But if it should turn out that they're filled with goods from the inn, wouldn't we look silly reporting it to the police?"

"I'll do a little more checking," Nancy agreed. "Let's get back to town."

After eating the delicious picnic lunch Bess had

prepared, Nancy drove her friend home, then went straight to her father's office. Through people he contacted she learned that at the time the Blue Iris Inn was sold, all the furnishings had been disposed of at auction. She asked his advice about telling the police her suspicions.

"Well, actually you haven't much to go on," he said. "Find out first whether Tombar himself bought some of the furnishings at the auction."

Nancy set off for the auctioneer's shop. A short distance from it she met Mr. Lightner.

"I'm glad I ran into you, Miss Drew," he declared cordially. "After you left my office I was trying to reach you by telephone."

"I've been for a ride in the country."

"I've arranged for you to attend the party this evening. It's to be a masquerade. What would you like to wear?" He added, smiling, "Lightner's costumes are at your disposal."

"How about my being a maid in the women's cloakroom?"

"Very good. A splendid place for scrutinizing guests. Come with me now and I'll find an outfit for you."

Nancy decided to postpone her call to the auctioneer's office. At the entertainment company she selected a well-tailored black dress with white collar and cuffs and a dainty ruffled cap.

"I have some news for you," Mr. Lightner said,

walking with Nancy to the front door. "I'm taking Linda Seeley back."

"Oh, I'm so glad!"

To have Linda reinstated in the firm was a great relief to Nancy. Nevertheless, if the series of thefts which had damaged the company's reputation continued, Linda might be blamed again.

"That makes this party tonight an important one," Nancy thought. "Oh, I do hope everything goes along without trouble!"

Upon arriving home Nancy was pleasantly surprised to find Ned Nickerson lounging on the porch.

"Schoolbooks are locked up," he joked.

"Ned! I'm glad to see you!"

"What's in the box? A new dress for a date with me tonight?"

"Maybe." Nancy told him of her plan to play the part of a maid at the Dwight party.

"How about coming with me? I think I could get you in as a checkroom boy. Want to help me catch a couple of masked thieves?"

"Well," Ned replied, "since you put it that way, the answer is, naturally, yes. But what do I know about checking men's hats or coats?"

"It's easy, and maybe you'll spot one of the Velvet Gang. I'll telephone Mr. Lightner."

Arrangements were made for Ned to obtain a uniform and assist the regular checker.

"Now bring me up to date on the recent happenings," Ned urged Nancy. "Remember, we didn't have a chance to talk alone on Friday night."

Rapidly she related how the thefts threatened Mr. Lightner's company with ruin. She told him about Peter Tombar and Ralph Snecker, and their apparent association.

"I'm inclined to think that both of them are mixed up in the thefts," she concluded. "The Velvet Gang may be working with them. At any rate, I want to investigate the Blue Iris Inn further."

"I'm surprised that you and George haven't been out there tearing the place apart board by board," Ned remarked, grinning.

At mention of George's name, Nancy sobered and told him of their friend's unhappy state of mind.

"Her parents are worried and so am I," she said. "We can't understand what's wrong."

"I'm sorry to hear that," Ned said.

He went home to dinner but was back at the Drews' by seven o'clock.

"You're a very handsome checkroom boy!" Nancy declared when she saw him in his uniform. "How do I look?"

"Lovely, but not natural. What a hairdo!"

"I had to disguise myself as much as I could."

"Be careful tonight, both of you," Mr. Drew

advised as the couple left the house. "I'll wait up until you're home safe."

Mr. Lightner, who had arrived early, was waiting for Nancy. He whispered that every precaution had been taken to avert another robbery and no trouble was expected.

"Six plainclothesmen are here to watch the guests. Nothing can go wrong."

Nancy and Ned were assigned to separate cloakrooms upstairs. Nancy found herself paired with a rather indifferent maid named Hilda.

"All we have to do is stay here and help the ladies with their things," the girl told Nancy. "Just don't get the stuff mixed up, that's all."

For the next hour Nancy checked guests' belongings efficiently, and quickly hung them on racks. Many of the costumes worn were very lovely and she recognized some as having been rented from Lightner's. Masks were of every form and shape. Nancy could not identify anyone.

After the dancing had started in the ballroom below, Mr. Lightner came upstairs. He informed Nancy that no guest had appeared without a properly marked admission card.

Relieved that no suspicious person had been observed, Nancy relaxed a little. Hilda stretched out comfortably on a lounge.

"We'll have a few hours now with nothing to do," she advised Nancy. "Take it easy before the rush starts."

Nancy preferred remaining alert and was standing near the door when a tall man in a striking costume came up and presented a check.

"Madam needs her coat," he said in low tones. "A long dark-green one. Hurry, please."

Nancy glanced intently at the stranger. She could not see his face plainly, for a white silk scarf that matched his Moorish costume served to mask the lower portion. His intense black eyes disturbed her, however.

She knew the coat he meant without comparing the numbered tickets, for there was no other like it. Deliberately she took her time, pretending she could not find the garment.

"Hurry!" the man urged again, speaking with a slight British accent.

More suspicious than ever that he was the thief she had previously encountered, Nancy purposely turned her back and maneuvered to run her hand into the inner pocket of the coat. Instantly her fingers encountered something made of cloth and very soft.

She quickly took out the object. It was one of the masks used by the daring members of the Velvet Gang! After tucking the velvet hood back in the pocket, she took the coat from the hanger and handed it to the man. With a suggestion of a French accent, she inquired:

"Madame is ill? She is leaving the party so soon? Perhaps I can help her?"

"No thanks," he replied, still keeping his face muffled in the white scarf. "I'll attend to her."

As soon as he was gone, Nancy told the dumbfounded Hilda, "You're in charge here alone now."

Unmindful of the maid's protests, Nancy hurried down the hall in pursuit of the man carrying the green coat. Passing the room where Ned was stationed, she gave him a prearranged signal. Immediately he joined her at the stairway.

"What's up?" he asked quickly.

"Keep an eye on that man in the Moor's costume," Nancy whispered. "No matter what happens, don't let him escape you."

From the staircase, the couple saw him move directly to a bent, white-haired old lady with glasses, who was waiting in the hallway below. She was not costumed.

Nancy and Ned watched intently as the man solicitously helped the woman put on her coat. Then they parted, the man turning toward the dance floor, and his companion moving slowly toward the entrance at the side of the house.

"Follow him, Ned!" Nancy whispered excitedly. "I'll watch her."

Ned started off in pursuit. The man dodged in and out among the dancers, and finally headed toward the kitchen. He pushed open the swinging door and darted inside.

Determined not to lose track of the man, Ned

also slipped through the door. He found himself in a large pantry and caught sight of his quarry disappearing through a door that apparently led to the basement.

Heedless of possible danger, Ned hurried across the kitchen. Reaching the entrance to the cellar, he opened the door and peered down the steps, at the same time flicking the basement light switch. The cellar remained dark. The man must have removed the bulb, Ned thought, in order to hamper pursuit and allow time to escape through the basement exit.

Lighting a match, Ned cautiously descended the stairs, looking for the fugitive. He was not in sight.

By the time Ned reached the bottom step, the match was burning his fingers and he dropped it. As he started to light another, Ned felt a thud, then a searing pain in his temple. The blow sent him sprawling on the cement floor, his head throbbing. He had been ambushed!

CHAPTER XV

Captured!

WHERE was the prowler? Ned reflected dizzily. Rising to his knees, he saw the beam of a flashlight far across the expansive basement. The dim figure holding the light was studying the electricity panel.

"He's going to pull the switch and plunge the whole house into darkness so the Velvet Gang can rob the place!" Ned thought. "I must stop him!"

Although his knees sagged, Ned pulled himself to his feet and crept toward his enemy. The man's hand reached for the switch. Ned sprang at his quarry, but a split second too late. The switch was pulled as the two went down in a tangled heap, rolling on the hard cement floor.

The struggle was a desperate one. Ned had but one purpose in mind: to knock out this muscular, wily opponent so that he could switch the lights on again. The other was as fiercely bent on keeping Ned pinned to the floor.

Meanwhile, Nancy had concentrated on the white-haired woman. Following at a careful distance, she observed the agile way the old lady walked when she thought she was not being noticed.

"That getup is a disguise, I'm sure," Nancy told herself. "In fact, that woman has the same figure as the one who was at both the Hendricks' party and the musicale at the Elkins' home."

It became apparent to Nancy that the woman knew exactly where she was going. The "old lady" stepped quickly past the side entrance and turned into a hallway.

With a sharp intake of breath, Nancy recalled that farther down the hall a priceless silver peacock was displayed on a table in front of a gilt mirror.

"I must catch her before she can steal it!"

Nancy stealthily drew closer to her quarry. But a creaking board beneath the thick broadloom carpet betrayed her presence. The woman turned swiftly to look over her shoulder. Seeing Nancy, she was so startled she forgot to maintain her bent position and straightened abruptly.

Nancy lunged forward to seize the thief. But she snatched only empty air. With amazing agility the woman side-stepped her. Just then the lights went off throughout the house.

Spurred by a realization that the thieves were about to score again, Nancy groped frantically for the "old lady." But suddenly she froze as a man's voice behind her commanded:

"Stand where you are! Don't move!"

Nancy immediately recognized the voice as that of Detective Ambrose. He had mistaken her for one of the thieves!

Ignoring his order to stand still, she kept feeling her way forward and groping for the elusive "old lady."

"She'll head straight for that silver peacock," Nancy reasoned, "so that's where I'll go."

In the darkness Nancy stumbled into the woman and quickly seized her.

"Let me go!" hissed the thief, clawing at her.

"Help!" cried Nancy, trying to hold the woman, who fought like a tigress!

Just then the lights went on. Detective Ambrose was running down the hall toward Nancy and her captive, a green-cloaked figure in a black velvet mask.

"Hang on!" Ambrose shouted.

"She has the peacock!" Nancy cried as the prisoner vainly tried to hide the long-tailed silver bird beneath her coat.

The detective seized the masked woman and

held her firmly while Nancy retrieved the valuable ornament. Then she pulled off the velvet hood.

Nancy had expected to expose the Javanese masquerader from the Hendricks' party. Instead, she faced the sullen-looking young woman who had assisted in George's abduction.

"One less masked thief!" Detective Ambrose exclaimed. "Where are the rest of them?"

The woman did not answer. After a moment the detective snapped a pair of handcuffs on her.

"Come along, sister," he said.

Meanwhile, Nancy had glimpsed something white sticking out from behind a nearby cabinet. She pulled out the wig which the masquerader had been wearing.

Before Nancy could tell the detective about it, Mrs. Dwight, accompanied by Mr. Lightner, came hastily down the hall. Both had been fearful of trouble when the lights went out.

"What happened?" Mr. Lightner demanded.

Mrs. Dwight who looked faint said nothing.

"Well, I guess we've got to give Miss Drew credit," the detective said. "She caught the thief!"

"Very fine," said Mr. Lightner. "What I want to know is how this woman got in here."

Nancy held up the wig. "She was wearing this. Did you admit a white-haired lady?"

Mrs. Dwight hastened to explain about the invitation to the woman she had never seen.

"Help!" cried Nancy, trying to hold the thief

"It was this way," she said apologetically. "Miss Wilkins, one of the invited guests, called me early this morning to ask if she could bring her elderly aunt and uncle. I told her yes, but explained the necessity for them to have properly marked invitations."

"You sent the extra ones?" Nancy asked.

"Yes, by special messenger. I marked the invitations myself," Mrs. Dwight admitted. "It was a mistake, I realize now, but I know Miss Wilkins well. I had no reason to distrust her."

Mrs. Dwight at once sought Miss Wilkins among the guests. The young woman immediately denied knowing the prisoner. Furthermore, she asserted she had no aunt nor uncle who had requested invitations.

"Just as I suspected," Ambrose declared. "This woman is a smart cooky. She used Miss Wilkins's name to get marked invitations."

During the questioning of the prisoner, plainclothesmen had been searching the grounds. Now one of them reported to the detective that none of the gang had been found.

Nancy spoke up. "This woman wasn't working alone. A man was with her. He was probably the 'uncle.' I talked to him. Oh, where did he go?"

Suddenly the group was startled by the unexpected appearance in the hallway of a disheveled Ned Nickerson. His uniform was torn, his face bruised, and his hair mussed.

"Ned!" Nancy cried in dismay. "You've been in a fight!"

"And how! That fellow you assigned me to follow proved to be a tough customer."

"He got away?"

"Yes," Ned admitted. "I could have held him, but I had a choice between turning the lights on or letting him go. I thought by switching them on I might stop a robbery up here."

"And you did," Nancy informed him. "If the lights hadn't gone on just when they did, I'm sure this woman would have escaped."

Ned told of the fight in the basement. His story was interrupted by Detective Ambrose.

"That's funny! We had a man posted down there to watch the lights. What became of him? Mack wouldn't leave his job."

Alarmed, Detective Ambrose turned his prisoner over to a plainclothesman and dashed to the basement. Nancy, Ned, Mr. Lightner, and Mrs. Dwight followed him.

The detective entered every room. As he opened the door of the cold-storage section, he uttered a startled exclamation. On the floor, unconscious, lay the missing Mack.

Though apparently the man had not been struck on the head, it took the detective a long while to revive him. When the plainclothesman recovered his senses, he said he had been attacked from the rear. Before Mack could fight off his assailant he had been drugged. Evidently this had been some time before Ned's arrival.

"That's the Velvet Gang's method," Nancy said to Mrs. Dwight.

"It's perfectly dreadful!" the woman said.

While waiting for the police car to arrive, Detective Ambrose said to his prisoner, "You're entitled to a lawyer, of course, while being questioned, but you may as well come clean and tell us how many are in the gang."

The woman's lips curled insolently. "Try and find out."

After she had been taken away, both Mrs. Dwight and Mr. Lightner complimented Nancy for her quick thinking and prompt action. They also thanked Ned for his part in the affair. Due to the efficient work of the young couple, not a single valuable object had been stolen.

"I only wish I'd caught that man," Ned said ruefully.

He and Nancy remained at the party another hour, thoroughly enjoying themselves as guests this time. But the mystery was their chief topic of conversation.

Ned declared with satisfaction, "Well, we've made a start toward clipping the wings of that gang!"

"Maybe. Friday is the test."

"Why Friday, Nancy?"

"It's the final date that was marked on the lining of the hooded mask."

"But after tonight you don't think the Velvet Gang will dare—"

"They'd dare anything, Ned! But what really bothers me is that so far as I know no important party is scheduled for that night."

"Then you haven't a single clue as to where something may happen?"

"Not one, Ned. And I'm afraid that the gang has set Friday as the day for a big robbery. Oh, if I only knew some way to stop it!"

CHAPTER XVI

Important Identification

As Nancy and Ned were saying good night later, he laughed. "You'll make a detective out of me yet, Nancy Drew." Then he became serious. "Here's an idea. Who is it that the gang is afraid of?"

"The police, of course."

"That's where you're wrong," Ned said. "It was Nancy Drew they tried to kidnap, not Chief McGinnis."

Nancy smiled. "Yes. Go on."

"It was you who caught that woman this evening. The gang will lie low for a while if you're around. But if you disappear they'll come out of hiding and the police can capture them." Ned grinned from ear to ear. "Which will leave you free for the big evening—to give me your entire attention."

Nancy laughed. "To think I fell for that! You win, Ned. Only—"

"No *if's* or *but's*. I have tickets for a picnic and dance some of my local fraternity brothers are giving."

Nancy assured Ned that she wanted to attend the party. "But if I should run into a clue that I had to follow up, you wouldn't mind, would you?"

"You're a hound for punishment," Ned teased. "Oh, well, if you do get a chance to crack the case, count me in. Another black eye won't matter. And something else. No work Wednesday or Thursday. Wednesday we go to the yacht club races and Fourth of July belongs to your dad, he told me."

"I'll remember."

Early the next morning Nancy telephoned the police captain and learned that the prisoner still refused to talk. She suggested bringing Linda Seeley to headquarters to see if the girl could identify her. It was possible that at some time the woman might have called at the Lightner Entertainment Company or attended one of the parties they had arranged.

Hopefully Nancy picked up Linda at her office. The chief of police had them conducted to the prisoner. Nancy watched closely to see if she recognized Linda. The girl detective was sure that the woman did, but the sign was so slight that Nancy did not bother to mention it.

"Have you changed your mind about talking to the police?" Nancy asked her.

The only response was a hateful glare. Then the woman turned her back. The girls returned to Chief McGinnis's office.

"I'm sure I've seen your prisoner before," Linda reported.

"Where?" he asked.

"Unless my memory is playing a trick on me, she was in Mr. Lightner's office to see about a party. She never gave it, though."

"She talked to Mr. Lightner?" Nancy asked.

"No. To Mr. Tombar. Mr. Lightner was away, but Mr. Tombar used his private office. Soon after the woman came in he sent me on an errand."

"So that you couldn't hear their conversation," Nancy surmised.

Chief McGinnis was very much interested in this bit of information. He suggested that perhaps Linda could identify something found on the prisoner. Detectives had questioned her several times since her arrest without the slightest success. Not a single clue as to her real identity had been obtained, and every tag had been removed from her clothing.

"But our policewoman did find this," the chief

said, taking a piece of unusual jewelry from his desk drawer.

"Oh yes, that bracelet came from Lightner's," Linda told him. "We rent it to go with a Turkish costume."

"You've been a great help, Misss Seeley," the chief said. "Maybe now that woman will talk."

The girls waited to hear the result, but it was negative. She still would admit nothing.

Nancy was tempted to tell the chief her suspicions about the numerous crates at the Blue Iris Inn. But realizing that she must have more specific evidence before accusing Tombar, she merely said:

"Chief McGinnis, if I should need some police assistance to do a little investigating during the next few days can you arrange it?"

"Certainly. Any time, and thanks for your help so far," Chief McGinnis said. "By the way," he added, "we questioned Snecker about the stolen miniature. Naturally he insists that he doesn't know how it got into the store. We're keeping our eye on him anyhow."

"I'm sure he'll bear watching," Nancy agreed.

The girls left headquarters and Nancy drove Linda back to work. On a hunch she asked for Tombar's address and went to his house. As she had suspected, it was vacant, and a neighbor told her that he and his wife had moved away rather unexpectedly.

"Do you have his forwarding address?" Nancy asked, thinking that Tombar's sudden departure looked like an admission of guilt.

"No, I don't. They went at night and didn't even say good-by."

"This is my unlucky day," Nancy reflected gloomily.

Her next stop was at Taylor's Department Store where she talked to the young clerk in the receiving-and-marking department. He assured her that Mr. Snecker was back at work. At the moment, however, he was away from the store, delivering merchandise in one of the trucks.

"I didn't know anyone in your department is supposed to do that," Nancy said.

"We don't usually," the clerk answered. "But when Mr. Snecker's asthma gets bad, he likes to get out, so he sometimes drives in place of a man who's taking the day off."

Nancy did not comment but she wondered if the manager of Taylor's knew about this.

"Will Mr. Snecker be here in the department tomorrow?" she inquired.

"No. He's going to take an extra long Fourth-of-July holiday, and is starting on a trip this evening. In fact, he won't be back after work today."

Nancy was greatly disappointed. She did not want to discontinue work on the case. But with dates of her own and a Fourth-of-July celebration with her father, there was no chance for further sleuthing until Friday.

But on Friday morning she discovered that Taylor's Department Store, as well as many other businesses in town, was closed. She walked to the office of the auctioneer to inquire whether Mr. Tombar had bought any of the furnishings of the Blue Iris Inn. But she found that it would not open until Monday.

"Anyway, I can ride out to the old inn and look around there again," Nancy thought. "I'll be back in plenty of time to dress for the picnic tonight. I wonder if Bess would go along. But first I'll stop to see how George is."

Bess was there, reading to her cousin. George appeared wan and unhappy.

"My, I'm glad you came, Nancy!" Bess exclaimed. "George has been frightfully worried that something might have happened to you."

"To me! What an idea!" Nancy laughed it off.

"I worry every minute that you'll get into real danger," George confessed.

"Why, I've been so good lately it hurts," Nancy replied. She still could not understand her friend's strange attitude.

Quickly Nancy steered the conversation away from the mystery. But secretly the young detective was eager to get to work. After a while she glanced at her watch.

"Where are you going now, Nancy?" George asked anxiously.

"I was thinking of a little ride into the country to a place called the Blue Iris Inn."

"Oh no—please don't! Bess told me about it."

"I couldn't help it, Nancy," Bess spoke up quietly. "George wormed it out of me."

"You mustn't go there alone, Nancy," George said urgently.

Bess said quickly, "I'll go with you, Nancy, if you want me to."

George twisted her hands nervously. "Don't do it!" she pleaded. "Anything you girls might learn isn't worth the risk."

Bess and Nancy tried to soothe their chum.

"Besides," Nancy declared reassuringly, "it'll have to be a short trip. I must be back soon to keep a date with Ned. We're going to a picnic some of his fraternity brothers are giving."

Later, while driving toward the inn, they discussed George's bewildering attitude.

"I wish the doctors could find out what's wrong with her," Nancy said.

"What if she never gets better?" Bess asked in a trembling voice.

"Don't suggest such a thing!" Nancy chided.

The next moment she noted a green sedan some distance ahead. Warily, she slowed down.

Soon the girls neared the old inn. The car

ahead turned into the driveway. Nancy wondered if Tombar was in it.

"Oh, we can't stop there now!" Bess exclaimed in alarm. "We'll be spotted if we do."

"I'll drive past and park," she told Bess. "We must walk back without being seen. I want to get a look at that driver."

A moment later the girls sighted the car parked near a side entrance of the Blue Iris Inn. As they passed, a man slipped from behind the wheel.

"Peter Tombar!" Nancy exclaimed softly. "If he's here for the reason I think he is, maybe this will turn out to be my luckiest day yet! Get ready, Bess! We must do some sleuthing."

CHAPTER XVII

Prisoners

HOPING Tombar had not seen them, Nancy drove a few hundred yards up the road from the Blue Iris Inn. She parked in the shelter of a clump of willows and the two friends tramped back to the deserted building.

"You won't go too close, promise," Bess begged.

"Just close enough to do some looking. We'll find out what Tombar's up to."

The green sedan still stood on the weed-choked driveway, but Peter Tombar was not in sight.

"He must be inside," Nancy said.

"If he catches us prowling around here, we may run into that danger George predicted!" Bess declared uneasily.

"Now don't get jittery," Nancy begged. "We'll stay out of sight."

Using the pine shrubbery as a shield, the girls

slipped to the side of the inn next to the driveway. Nancy made her way cautiously through the shrubbery to a boarded window.

"You keep watch," she told Bess, and peered through a tiny crack.

"What do you see?" her friend demanded in an impatient whisper. "Is Tombar in there?"

"Someone's moving around with a flashlight. Yes, it's Tombar all right! But all the crates and cartons are gone!"

"You've seen everything you can," Bess whispered, tugging at her friend's hand. "Come on!"

Nancy held back. In fascination she watched as Peter Tombar lifted a trap door in the floor of the empty room and disappeared below.

"I can't leave now," Nancy whispered. "I wonder what is in the cellar."

"Come away, Nancy!" Bess warned. "A truck is turning in here!"

It was too late for the girls to retreat to the road without being seen. They flattened themselves against the boarded side window, hoping not to be observed.

Luck was with them, for instead of coming all the way up the drive, the covered truck halted near the road. As the girls anxiously waited, it backed up again and drove away.

"A Taylor company truck!" Nancy exclaimed. "And the store's closed today!"

"The driver saw us!" Bess insisted fearfully.

"Maybe not," Nancy replied. "Anyway, we'll have time to see if Tombar brings up anything from the cellar."

"Let's go now," Bess urged nervously.

Nancy ignored her friend's plea. Squinting through the crack again, she waited patiently.

Soon she saw Mr. Tombar emerge through the trap door. He carried something in his hands.

"Oh, that proves it!" Bess whispered tensely. "Tombar is part of the gang!"

"He's probably one of the ringleaders," Nancy replied. "They're going to use those masks tonight!"

Bess put her eye to the crack, too. She became so absorbed in watching that she forgot her job as lookout. The girls were suddenly awakened to their danger when Tombar started toward the side door.

"Let's leave, Nancy," Bess urged. "We may be too late to—"

The sentence was never finished. Nancy heard a crackle back of them. She whirled to face a man and a woman wearing black velvet masks. As Bess screamed, the two threw dark hoods over the girls' heads. Strong arms seized them. Struggling frantically, Nancy almost broke away when crashing sounded in the brush and someone else grabbed her.

"What is it? Who are they?" came Peter Tombar's harsh voice.

"The Drew girl and her friend," the woman reported.

"So!" Tombar exclaimed. "I know Nancy Drew has been spying on me for days. We'll deal with her presently. Right now, get 'em both out of the way. Harris is coming and I don't want him to see 'em."

Nancy and Bess were hustled into the inn and taken down into the dark, musty cellar. There the hoods were exchanged for blindfolds, and the girls were bound and gagged.

"You see what happens to people who don't mind their own business?" Tombar taunted as he ascended the stairs.

Though the captives could not speak, see, or move, they could hear plainly what went on in the rooms above. Presently the real-estate man arrived and was greeted cordially by Tombar.

"I'm glad you drove out today, Mr. Harris," he said courteously. "I've been thinking over your client's offer to buy this place."

"Then you'll sell?"

"If the price is right, and we can make a quick deal. My wife is tired of River Heights. We want to travel. It will have to be an immediate cash sale, though, or it's all off."

"Give me a couple of hours," Mr. Harris replied. "I think I can swing it."

"Okay. I'll meet you at your office."

Lying on the dusty, damp cellar floor, Nancy

unhappily considered her predicament. Mr. Tombar intended to sell the inn and leave River Heights with his cronies before the police caught up with them.

If only she and Bess could escape and bring state troopers there in time to thwart their plan! But the girls' bonds were secure and there was no chance of loosening them.

"And maybe no one will find us," Nancy reflected despairingly as she heard Harris's car leave.

Only George Fayne knew where she and Bess had gone. Formerly their failure to return to River Heights in a reasonable length of time would have signaled trouble. But now George was not herself. Could she possibly be depended upon to send help? Nancy wondered.

Twenty minutes elapsed, then the girls heard footsteps on the cellar stairs. Their ankles were unbound and they were pulled roughly to their feet.

"Come along," a man said gruffly. "You're going to be moved."

The girls' hearts sank. Their one chance of rescue was vanishing!

"Unless," Nancy thought, "our rescuers could pick up our trail."

As the girls were prodded up the stairway, Nancy pondered how she might leave a clue. She thought of the buttons on her dress. Could she possibly get one off?

Stumbling sideways against the wall, she deliberately tried to tear one off. Luck favored her. A protruding nail ripped her dress. She heard a button drop on the step!

"It's a slight hope," she thought as her captor yanked her around again.

"Keep goin'," he ordered. "No stallin'." When they reached the main floor of the inn, he said, "Okay, Pete."

"You two get those girls out of here," Tombar ordered. "And make it snappy."

The girls' ankles were bound again. Their arms still tied behind them, and with gags and blindfolds in place, they were lifted into a vehicle and put on the floor. The driver started the motor and pulled away at high speed. Nancy and Bess wondered if they were in the Taylor truck they had seen backing out of the driveway.

As they rode along, the girls could hear the couple in the front seat talking. Nancy was sure they were speaking in disguised voices.

"If I can catch them off guard," she thought, "maybe they'll speak in natural tones."

Nancy thumped her feet up and down.

"Florence, what's that?" the man cried.

"The detective's up to her tricks again."

Florence Snecker's voice! Was the companion

her husband? He did not sound like the man whose voice she had heard in the apartment.

"You girls keep quiet or you'll be sorry," the woman warned. "We don't want no trouble with you!"

Nancy smiled inwardly. She had achieved her purpose, but as to making trouble, what chance did she have?

"But I mustn't give up hope," Nancy chided herself.

She wondered about Bess who had made no move. Had she fainted?

The two girls were at opposite ends of the truck. Nancy tried to reach Bess but the effort was too painful. She longed for the journey to end.

Presently the truck slowed down. They must be in a town. After turning several corners, it finally stopped. The motor was switched off. Apparently the truck was in some back alley, for there were no street noises. Nancy heard the woman remark to her male companion:

"I'm glad our friend's going to Harris instead of waiting for him at the inn. He used good sense to unload on Harris and pull out. This town's getting too hot for all of us."

Nancy felt certain that Mrs. Snecker was speaking of Peter Tombar. If so, it meant that he would flee the city as soon as he had collected the cash from the real-estate agent. The police

would not find him, even if it occurred to George
Fayne to send them to the inn to investigate.

The girls were hauled out of the truck, untied,
and forced to walk into a building. There they
were made to sit on the floor while their ankles
were rebound.

"Good-by, snooper," Mrs. Snecker said, giving
Nancy a vicious prod with her shoe. "Now let's
see you tell the police what you know!"

The man added, "We'll soon take you away to
a place where you'll never squeal!"

A heavy door was rolled shut and locked. The
room became silent.

Nancy squirmed and twisted but she could
not loosen the cords which held her prisoner.
Seldom had she been in a more hopeless situa-
tion!

She was certain now that Peter Tombar and
the Sneckers were working together in the Velvet
Gang. They meant to pull one final robbery and
flee.

But what good was this knowledge? She was
unable to notify the police or even to free herself and Bess.

"Oh, why did I let myself get caught!" Nancy
scolded herself.

CHAPTER XVIII

A Threat Revealed

In River Heights the long absence of Nancy and Bess had begun to cause alarm. Hannah Gruen knew something had gone wrong because Nancy had not returned to dress for her date with Ned. Frantic with worry she had telephoned the Marvin home several times but had always received the same answer—there had been no word from Bess.

At seven o'clock Ned arrived. Hearing that Nancy had not come home, he frowned in concern.

"I was afraid of this. She becomes so completely wrapped up in a mystery. Now something's happened." He began pacing the floor.

"Mr. Drew won't be home until late," Hannah informed him. "I've tried to reach him by phone but I can't. I don't know what to do about Nancy and Bess."

Tearfully she disclosed that the two girls had been seen last at the Fayne home. At that time they had told George that they might drive out to a place called the Blue Iris Inn.

"But nobody seems to know where it is. The inn's not listed in the phone book."

"I never heard of the place until Nancy mentioned it," Ned admitted. "And she didn't say where it was."

"Oh, Ned, can't you think of something we can do?" the housekeeper pleaded.

"I'll go out to the inn as soon as I find out where it is," the young man promised. "Maybe George can give me a clue."

He drove at once to the Fayne home. George was up and dressed, but in a near state of collapse from anxiety over the girls' disappearance.

"Oh, I knew this would happen!" George moaned. "I warned Bess and Nancy not to go, but they wouldn't listen to me. Now the dreadful threat may be carried out."

"Threat?" Ned demanded. "What threat, George?"

"Tell us quickly!" Mrs. Marvin urged. "Nancy and Bess's safety may depend on what you can tell us."

The words stunned George and suddenly brought a marked change in her attitude. The old fire came back into her eyes and the color returned to her cheeks.

"Well," George began, "after those kidnappers drugged me I seemed to lose my nerve. That woman's words just burned into my brain. She warned me that if I didn't make Nancy drop the case, great harm would come not only to her but to Mrs. Gruen and Mr. Drew and my family and Bess's."

"Oh, George, you should have reported this to the police," Mrs. Fayne cried.

"I didn't dare. But now we must find Nancy and Bess."

"What else did the kidnappers say?" Ned asked. "It might be a clue to what happened to Nancy and Bess."

"Well, at the end of the threats, the woman said, 'We'll put Nancy on ice in the flour cellar!' I've wondered ever since what they meant by that."

"A flour cellar?" Mrs. Marvin murmured. "What significance would that have?"

"I never heard of a flour mill around here," Ned said thoughtfully. "George, maybe they meant f-l-o-w-e-r cellar."

"That might have been it," she agreed. "Do you suppose there's one in the Blue Iris Inn? Wait! Nancy told me about a real-estate agent who has been wanting to buy that place for someone. I'll ask him."

Excitedly, and now apparently completely recovered, George ran to the telephone and called Mr. Harris. When she rejoined the group in the living room, her face was worried but determined.

"I've learned a lot," she said. "Mr. Harris told me the inn once had a small greenhouse specializing in blue iris. The cellar of the inn was used for sorting bulbs and arranging cut flowers."

"Nancy and Bess probably are prisoners in that cellar!" Ned cried. "But where is it?"

"Mr. Harris gave me directions," George replied. "And listen to this. He also told me that he had arranged today to buy the inn from Mr. Tombar for a client."

"Tombar! Nancy suspected him all along," Ned cried.

"Mr. Harris was supposed to have paid Tombar at his office, but he had trouble raising the money on such short notice, so he told Tombar to return Monday."

"Maybe Tombar went back to the inn!" Ned exclaimed. "If he did, we can catch him and find out about the girls!"

"I'm going too," George announced with spirit. "No, don't try to stop me, anyone! Nancy and Bess are in danger, and I want to help."

The rescue party, Ned, Mr. Marvin, George, and her father, assembled quickly. As they were ready to drive off, Mrs. Gruen telephoned that she finally had reached Mr. Drew.

"He has notified the State Police and is on his way to the inn himself right now," she said. "Oh, get there as fast as you can!"

At the Blue Iris Inn, Ned's party learned from Mr. Drew that Nancy's parked car as well as tire tracks of a truck and another car had been found. The officers had broken into the boarded-up building and searched in vain for the missing girls.

"Let me look," Mr. Drew said, borrowing a flashlight from one of the policemen.

It was not until he went to the cellar of the inn that Mr. Drew found a clue. He pointed out that some of the footprints on the stairway had been made by the type of shoes Nancy wore.

"And look at this!" George exclaimed, picking up the button that had fallen off Nancy's dress. "This was on the dress Nancy was wearing when she disappeared!"

"Now we have something to work on," one officer said excitedly. "No doubt the girls were taken away from here in the car or the truck. We'll try to trace the tire tracks."

By inspecting the marks the police figured that the truck and the car, leaving the inn, had gone toward River Heights.

"They came from that same direction, too," remarked one of the troopers.

"It'll be impossible to follow the tracks on the highway," another pointed out.

"The best thing to do is broadcast a general

"This was on the dress Nancy was wearing when she disappeared!"

alarm for Tombar's green car," Mr. Drew declared. "You may be able to stop it somewhere."

"We'll do everything we can," the officer promised. "But the girls may be in the truck and we have no description of that. And don't forget, those thieves have a good head start. They may be a hundred miles from here by now."

"On the other hand, they may be only a few miles away," Ned put in. "Nancy believed that the Velvet Gang planned to pull a last big job tonight. If she's right, they won't leave town until they have the loot."

"Her theory is a good one," the officer conceded. "It won't help us rescue her and Miss Marvin, though. By the time we get a report on the robbery, the gang will be on their way to another place."

"And taking Nancy and Bess with them!" George exclaimed.

"All the more reason why we must set up roadblocks," Mr. Drew urged. As he started for his car he noticed that Ned had remained behind.

"Hurry, Ned!" he called.

The young man shook his head. "I'm staying here. There's an outside chance that the gang may come back tonight."

"But we're trying to save the girls."

"They may bring Nancy and Bess with them."

"You're going to stay alone?" Mr. Drew said dubiously.

"I'll be okay," Ned insisted. "Maybe no one but Tombar will show up."

"But he may be armed, Ned," Mr. Drew pointed out. "It seems to me you're taking a dangerous chance. Better come along with us."

"I'll watch my step. I have two good fists," the athletic young man said grimly, "and I'm used to tackling opponents on short notice.

"What's more, if I ever meet that fellow who nailed me in the basement of the Dwight house, I have a score to settle with him!"

CHAPTER XIX

Fire!

In their prison room Nancy and Bess were suffering intense discomfort. Their gags made swallowing difficult, and the cords cut deeply into their flesh.

"Those men made a thorough job of seeing that we don't get away," Nancy thought grimly.

So tightly had her wrist bonds been tied, she realized that she could never unfasten them without aid. The ropes about her ankles were somewhat looser, but it was impossible to reach them.

"I'll wiggle around and perhaps I'll find something to help me get them off," Nancy thought eagerly. "But where is Bess?"

As she rolled and twisted on the floor, Nancy brushed against an object with a sharp edge. It seemed to be a loose metal band around a large box.

At once Nancy raised her bound feet and began to saw her bonds across the metal. It was hard work. Repeatedly she abandoned the task as fatigue overcame her. But after each rest period she tried again.

Finally she succeeded. The frayed ankle cords broke. Her feet were free!

Nancy scrambled up, and though she still could not see because of the blindfold, she groped backward with her tied hands until she found the sharp piece of metal. Another five minutes and both hands were free. She jerked off the blindfold and removed the gag.

"What a relief!" she gasped.

The unlighted prison was apparently windowless. Nancy was conscious of crates and boxes piled about her. Where was she?

Not knowing whether there was a guard nearby, Nancy did not dare call out Bess's name. She would have to find Bess by feeling her way around.

As she started her search, Nancy's forehead touched a string from an overhead, swinging light bulb. She switched it on.

The brightness revealed that she had been left captive in the shipping room of Taylor's Department Store. After a hunt in the aisles between the crates, she found Bess.

Quickly Nancy freed her friend and helped her to stand up. Bess found it difficult to walk because her legs had become numb.

"Where are we?" she asked in a whisper, her voice quavering with fright.

"In the receiving-and-marking room of Taylor's store."

"Let's get out!" Bess urged.

She hobbled to a heavy metal door at the far end of the room. It was locked!

"I was afraid of that," Nancy muttered. "Now—"

She quickly switched off the light, aware of voices on the other side of the heavy door.

Nancy tiptoed over and the girls pressed their ears against it and listened.

A man was talking, bragging about the ease with which the two girls had been captured. He reported that they were neatly tied up and ready for their second ride in another half hour.

"If we hadn't caught that Drew girl she might have interfered with us tonight. And nobody's goin' to stop me from takin' a big haul out of old man Taylor's store! Once we get the silver and the furs, we'll pick up those girls and beat it. And you are to come back here in ten minutes to be sure everything's okay."

Nancy's pulse began to pound. So the Velvet Gang was going to rob Taylor's Department Store! She must stop them! But how?

"Let's scream for help," Bess whispered.

"No, Bess! That would only bring them in here

to tie us up again. Maybe there's a telephone in this place."

The girls waited until they thought their captors had left, then turned on the light. Though they found a desk, there was no telephone on it.

"Now what'll we do?" Bess asked.

"Let's examine the walls for some sort of exit," Nancy suggested. "There may be a chute to shove boxes through. I want to find out what these cartons contain. This big carton looks exactly like one I saw at the Blue Iris Inn!"

"How would it get here?"

"Snecker uses a Taylor truck, don't forget. Furthermore, he's in charge of this room."

"But why would he bring the cartons here, Nancy? It doesn't make sense."

Nancy tore open the top of the box. The first item she lifted out was another miniature which had been stolen from the Hendricks.

As Bess examined the walls for a means of escape, Nancy went on with her task. Underneath some shredded tissue she found other things which she knew had been taken from her friend's home.

"I've found the loot!" Nancy excitedly told Bess, who had now reached the third wall without locating a door or chute.

"Wonderful! But that doesn't get us out of here."

Bess examined the fourth wall. No better luck. Nancy had opened two more cartons. Both contained stolen goods.

"But these boxes are all marked with the Taylor store name!" Bess said.

"To fool anyone who became curious. The thieves packed the stolen goods at the inn. Then Snecker or some of his helpers would bring them here. Snecker marked the cartons as damaged merchandise to be returned to the original shipper."

"The shippers are in the gang?"

"No. They're innocent. The boxes never reached them. You'll notice they are addressed to only two factories, both in distant cities. One of the gang must work in each factory. He takes the loot out and sells it to a pawnbroker or some other fence."

"All of these boxes and crates are being shipped by the thieves?" Bess gasped.

"Oh no. They couldn't get by with that. I think most of the boxes are incoming merchandise. See, here's one marked *Sweaters*."

"And here's another stamped *Porcelain*," Bess added. "That big one is marked *Toys*."

Curious to learn if the box actually contained toys, Nancy ripped open the top.

"Toys all right," she conceded. "Games, an atom bomb set, a chemical set and—say! This gives me an idea!"

"What?" Bess demanded eagerly.

"Maybe we'll get out of here yet!"

"Oh, I hope so. But how, Nancy?"

"This chemical set! See, one package is marked *Smoke!* By mixing the chemicals, we can make it appear that there's a fire here when one of the men returns."

"And maybe start a real one!" Bess worried.

"No danger of that, Bess. Listen at the door while I whip up a 'fire.' Maybe someone's out there now."

Bess pressed her ear against the steel door. She could hear a hum of voices. Then a man said, "It won't be long now. I'll be back in twenty minutes."

Now Bess could hear only one person moving around in the next room. She told Nancy.

"Good! My smoke preparation is ready. We'll see if it works. Get some rope and turn out the light."

Bess snatched up the cords, gag, and blindfold which had been used on her and then turned off the overhead light.

Crouching down on the floor by the locked door, Nancy began to blow smoke from the chemical set beneath the crack.

"We might yell 'Fire,'" Bess whispered, hopeful of quick action.

"Then he'd know we've taken off our gags, Bess. I want to surprise the guard."

Patiently Nancy kept blowing smoke under the door crack. Suddenly she was rewarded. From the other side of the door, the girls heard a startled exclamation.

"He's noticed the smoke!" Nancy murmured to Bess. "Stand back!"

Scarcely had the two girls flattened themselves against the wall when the metal door was unbolted and pushed back.

As the guard rushed in, looking about in bewilderment and sniffing the smoke-laden air, Nancy extended her foot directly in his path.

Down he went, sprawling full length on the floor!

CHAPTER XX

Unmasked

IN a flash Nancy and Bess seized the man's arms and legs and held him down. As he struggled, they quickly stuffed the gag in his mouth.

"Now we'll tie him up," said Nancy.

The girls bound the man's hands and ankles. Then Nancy switched on the light for a moment to look at the captive.

"I'm sure he was one of George's kidnappers!" she exclaimed. "Are you Ralph Snecker?" she asked him. "Nod yes or no!" He remained motionless, glaring at her.

She must find out! Nancy slipped one hand into his coat pocket and pulled out a wallet. Opening it, Nancy found a driver's license issued to Ralph Snecker.

The clerk's keys were handy. Nancy grabbed them.

"We must prevent the robbery if we can, Bess," she said. "Come on!"

The girls closed the heavy metal door behind them and tiptoed through an adjoining darkened room. Crossing the alley between the buildings, Nancy tried one key after another in the first door she came to. At last she found one that fit. She turned it and quietly let herself and Bess in.

"Do be careful," her friend urged. "There ought to be a night watchman around. Where is he?"

"I wish I knew."

The girls ascended a short flight of stairs and pushed a swinging door which opened into the first floor of the store.

Nancy and Bess moved forward in the dimly lighted building until the jewelry counter came to view. Two women and a man wearing velvet masks were looting the display cases of their valuable pieces!

"How dreadful!" Bess murmured. "What'll we do? We can't capture all three."

"With luck, we can," Nancy whispered. "We'll find a phone and call the police."

Quietly retreating, the girls located a telephone booth in the rear. Nancy called headquarters. She had hardly spoken her name when Chief McGinnis said:

"Where are you? There's a three-state alarm out for you!"

"In Taylor's. A robbery's going on. Come quickly! I'll meet you at the employees' entrance in the alley."

"We'll be right there!"

The girls crept back to see what was happening in the jewelry department. Time seemed to drag.

"I wish the police would hurry," Bess whispered uneasily. "If they don't get here soon—"

Just then the girls heard the wail of a police siren. The sound also reached the ears of the masked thieves.

"The cops!" exclaimed one of the women shrilly. "We've got to get out o' here!"

In a panic the three rushed for the employees' entrance. But Nancy and Bess had hurried to it ahead of them and blocked their way.

Seeing that escape was cut off, the man wheeled and ran in the opposite direction. The women made the mistake of trying to overpower Nancy and Bess.

They were still engaged in a fierce struggle when the police, led by Detective Ambrose, rushed up. Handcuffs were placed on both women.

"The man with them got away!" Nancy gasped. "But another—Ralph Snecker—is tied up in the shipping room."

Two officers started a search while a third removed the masks from the two women.

"Florence Snecker!" Nancy cried, recognizing one of them.

The other was the woman who had costumed herself as a Javanese beauty, and otherwise disguised her appearance. Both scowled at Nancy.

Though the police searched the store from roof to cellar, the only person they found was the night watchman, bound and gagged in the freight elevator. Snecker was brought from the shipping room, and the three prisoners were taken to the office of Mr. Taylor, who had been summoned by Ambrose.

The missing thief had stolen a quantity of jewelry, but Mr. Taylor estimated that Nancy and Bess had saved the store a huge loss.

"I can't thank you enough, Miss Drew. How did you ever trail these people?"

Nancy gave a brief account of the case, ending with, "I began to suspect Snecker when I found out he was a friend of Tombar. I wonder if the man who escaped could be Tombar."

Ambrose turned to his prisoners. "Is he?"

Silence.

Assisted by Nancy, who supplied much of the evidence, he questioned the three. At first they refused to talk, but Mrs. Snecker finally broke down. She gave a whining account of her part in the scheme which was mostly writing letters to a pawnshop dealer and another fence. This was her first burglary job, she insisted.

"If we're going to jail, so are the others!" Snecker burst out bitterly. "There are two men in this who are more guilty than we are."

"Tell your story," Detective Ambrose said. "First of all, what's the right name of that woman we're holding in jail?"

"Mrs. Ridley. She's Mrs. Snecker's half sister," the man answered sullenly. "She didn't join the gang until lately."

"And your name?" the detective questioned the second woman. She remained stubbornly silent.

"That's Ermintrude Schiff, an actress," Snecker informed him.

Snecker went on to place most of the blame on Peter Tombar, who, he said, had worked closely with Mrs. Snecker's brother, the man who had escaped from the store.

"What's his name?" Ambrose asked, jotting down the information Snecker had provided.

"Jerry Goff. He's well-educated, Jerry is. He uses an English accent sometimes to impress people."

"And also to disguise his voice," Nancy thought, recalling her adventure of being almost suffocated at one of the parties. Aloud she said, "Was he the man who wore the black cloak at the Hendricks' masquerade?"

"Yes, Tombar lent it to him. When you found a hole in it, Tombar took the cloak away in a hurry."

"This Jerry Goff was one of the men who helped with George Fayne's abduction, wasn't he?" Nancy asked.

"Yes. He sat in front of you."

"You were in on it, too, weren't you?" Nancy prodded.

"Yes," Snecker admitted. "I helped Mrs. Schiff. We muffed the job, getting the wrong girl." He said that Tombar's wife was not involved in any way.

"You also slipped up when you dropped your department-store charge plate from the car window."

"It flew from my breast pocket accidentally when I yanked out a handkerchief. It wouldn't have mattered except that you found it."

"Then you must have been the one who advised the store employees not to turn in their plates after the credit manager gave the order," Nancy remarked.

"Sure," Snecker said with a shrug. "I sent around a fake order. I knew I'd be caught if all the plates came in except mine."

Questioned further, Snecker identified Jerry Goff as the member of the gang who made friends with the servants and kitchen help at various parties. In this way he could slip unchallenged to the basement and switch off the lights.

"Jerry thought up the scheme in the first place and sold Tombar the idea," Snecker disclosed, "and Tombar pulled the rest of us into this mess."

"He planned all the robberies?" Nancy questioned.

"Every one. He gave us a list of the places we were to knock off, supplied masks and costumes, and room plans of the houses."

"And cards to admit you?"

"Oh, sure. Tombar thought of everything. He was pretty cool until you made the going tough for him, Miss Drew. Then he began to get nervous."

"Tell me how the stolen Marie Antoinette miniature got to the store's gift department," Nancy asked.

"It was a slip-up. The miniatures were at Tombar's hideout in the country. By mistake I put that one in my pocket and my helper saw it. I had to send it to the gift department then, and didn't dare recall it. I got flustered and marked it at a ridiculously low price."

Nancy next asked Snecker if he had any idea how Peter Tombar might be captured.

"He'll get out of town as quickly as he can," the clerk replied. "His job was to have the getaway car waiting for us around the corner. I guess he took off, though, when he heard the siren. But he may head back to the country to get some things he had stored in the inn."

With this full confession, the three prisoners

were escorted to headquarters to be booked on robbery and kidnapping charges. Bess and Nancy accompanied the officers to make a report on their part in the capture. While they were talking to Chief McGinnis, Mr. Drew hurried in with George, her father, and Mr. Marvin.

"Nancy! Bess!" George cried wildly. "You're safe!"

Information was exchanged hurriedly. When Nancy learned that Ned had remained at the Blue Iris Inn as guard in case one of the abductors should return, she became alarmed.

"We think Peter Tombar may go back there, especially if Goff gets word to him what happened in the store," Nancy told her father. "If Ned should be taken by surprise—"

"We'll return there right now," Mr. Drew broke in.

McGinnis added, "I'll notify the State Police to meet you there."

"I hope we're not too late," Nancy said as they left headquarters.

George insisted upon going, despite protests from Bess and Mr. Fayne.

"I feel fine," she insisted stubbornly. "Now that I know the Velvet Gang is nearly rounded up and Nancy safe, my worries are ended. This excitement tonight has cured me!"

"That's our old George!" Nancy declared happily, hugging her. "It sounds more natural to hear you talk that way."

At the Blue Iris Inn two troopers were waiting for them. Neither Ned nor the escaped leader of the party thieves was in evidence. Finding the rear door unlocked, they rushed in. A muffled shout reached them from the kitchen area.

"Come here!" Ned called. "I need help!"

Everyone rushed to the kitchen. The troopers' flashlights disclosed Peter Tombar pinned to the floor, with Ned sitting on his midriff.

"I'm sure glad you got here," the youth said in obvious relief. "I've been trying to figure out a way to get this guy to headquarters."

Relieved of his prisoner, Ned related how he had hidden in the old inn and watched through a crack between the boards on a front window. His wait had not been in vain. Tombar arrived in a black sedan which he parked up the road behind the willows.

"He sneaked in and went straight to the kitchen," Ned disclosed. "He had a lot of money in the cupboard under the sink. He was just reaching for the roll when I tackled him."

Tombar's clothing had been torn in the fight and one eye was blackened. Glaring at Nancy, he savagely berated her for the capture of the Velvet Gang. Still fuming, he was taken off by the troopers.

Later that night Goff was caught as he attempted to board a plane at the River Heights airport. Several days elapsed before Nancy and her friends were assured that the entire gang had been rounded up with the arrest of a pawnbroker in one city and a fence in another.

Dozens of cartons of silver and other valuables stolen from River Heights' homes were recovered and returned to their owners. In a few instances treasures already sold were traced.

One evening Mr. Lightner came to call personally to thank Nancy. "I value my reputation as much as I do my business," he told the young detective and her father. "And you saved both for me."

"Of course you will have no damage suits to defend," Carson Drew interposed with a smile, "so your troubles are really at an end."

Mr. Lightner beamed. "Again I say, I owe everything to Nancy."

At that moment Bess, George, and Ned arrived. After Mr. Lightner had been introduced, he told the trio why he was there at the Drews'.

"There's so little I can do to show my appreciation," he added. "But I'm giving Nancy a mask as a small token of my gratitude."

"Not a velvet hooded mask?" Nancy joked.

"No, indeed. We're through with those forever. I'm giving you an ancient mask of a beautiful Egyptian queen."

Mr. Lightner smiled and from a box took two identical masks. It was evident that one was very old, the other a new copy.

"How lovely!" Nancy exclaimed. "Thank you very much, Mr. Lightner. But why two of them?"

"One to treasure, one to wear at a masquerade."

"And that may be sooner than you think," Ned spoke up, grinning. "The fellows decided on another summer party—this time a masquerade. You'll go as an Egyptian queen."

"What fun!"

"Nancy ought to go as the Queen of Mystery," Bess remarked. "I'll bet it won't be long before she's in the midst of another case."

Bess's prophecy was to come true when Nancy set out to solve one of the most puzzling cases of her career, *The Ringmaster's Secret.*

"What are you girls going to wear to the masquerade?" she questioned Bess and George.

"You know me—always Bopeep." Bess giggled.

"I'll have to think it over," George replied. "But there's one person I know I'll never try to imitate."

"Who's that?" Bess asked.

"The well-known detective, Nancy Drew." George pretended to shiver. "I tried it once and found it too dangerous!"